THIS LAND IS MINE

Gemma has come from England to stay with her frail grandmother, who lives in the Oregon woods. Whilst shopping in the nearby town, Gemma gets into conversation with a lady called Sugar, who invites her to dinner at her home. There, she meets Sugar's ruggedly handsome brother, Grant. However, when her grandmother dies soon afterwards, Gemma learns that Grant's family has been pestering the old lady to sell them her land. Gemma now owns the property, but can she ever find happiness there?

Books by Mary Barham
in the Linford Romance Library:

LOVE ALL
BREATH OF FRESH AIR

MARY BARHAM

THIS LAND IS MINE

Complete and Unabridged

LINFORD
Leicester

First published in Great Britain

First Linford Edition
published 2002

British Library CIP Data

Barham, Mary
     This land is mine.—Large print ed.—
Linford romance library
1. Love stories
2. Large type books
I. Title
823.9'14 [F]

ISBN 0–7089–9813–5

Published by
F. A. Thorpe (Publishing)
Anstey, Leicestershire

Set by Words & Graphics Ltd.
Anstey, Leicestershire
Printed and bound in Great Britain by
T. J. International Ltd., Padstow, Cornwall

This book is printed on acid-free paper

1

The bright, blue bird that was perching on the branch of a fir tree a few feet away resembled an English kingfisher. Gemma caught her breath at its beauty. Her enthusiasm made her grandmother smile. Since Gemma had come to stay with her, the quiet of this lonely cabin deep in the Oregon woods had become charged with the vitality of youth.

'It's so brilliantly coloured. What is it?' Gemma asked.

'That's a scrub jay, honey,' Ruth Lawrence answered drily. As she spoke, the bird screeched, then flew off and was lost to sight amongst the tall, majestic trees surrounding the cabin.

Gemma's face fell when she heard it. 'It makes a horrid noise!'

'We don't like them much hereabouts. Down in California, they've got real jays. These are like those pesky squirrels and chipmunks, skittering round the house all day.'

Gemma leaned forward and took her grandmother's veined hand in her own, warm, young one.

'You've been here so long, you take all this beauty for granted. You can't imagine how it looks to a newcomer. The boys would love it here.'

The old woman's face lapsed into its customary grimness. Gemma sensed that she didn't want to be reminded of her granddaughter's home and family in England. The old lady's natural possessiveness meant that she wanted to keep her only living relative with her.

Gemma's father, Ruth Lawrence's only son, had died in England twenty-two years ago. Gemma's mother had eventually re-married and had a second, younger family. The connection had been only tenuously maintained but now, aware of her age and her frailty, old Mrs Lawrence had summoned her granddaughter to Oregon, sending the air ticket and a substantial sum of money.

Gemma urged, 'You'll have to come to England, and see us all when I get back. You'd enjoy meeting the boys, and I'd love to show you the country.'

The old woman snorted, brusquely removing her hand from Gemma's. 'No good talking about that. I'm not about to fly thousands of miles when there's little enough life left to me.'

'Don't talk like that. You've got years and years ahead of you. Now we're together, we're going to enjoy ourselves.'

'Of course we are.' The old woman was reassuring. 'There's no hurry for you to go back. I want you here, beside me.'

Gemma's brow puckered. This had been a constant theme since her arrival, and much as she now loved the place, she knew she had to leave sometime. Her mother and stepfather had made sacrifices to put her through college; she felt she must repay them by getting

3

a job although, at the moment, the thought of continuing living a peaceful life in this pine forest was alluring.

Ruth, looking at Gemma's bare feet, said, 'I've told you a million times, put some shoes on. You'll get splinters in your feet.'

'All right, Grandm-a-ah!' Gemma imitated an American drawl but went obediently through the open doors into the house.

Twenty minutes later, Gemma returned to the veranda with a tea tray in her hands. Seeing that her grandmother was asleep, she put it carefully down on the table beside her, as Ruth stirred and opened her eyes. 'I'm sorry, I didn't mean to wake you. I've made some tea and tomato sandwiches.'

'English ways again. What's wrong with some coffee and cinnamon rolls?'

Gemma grinned as she asked rather anxiously, 'Would you prefer that? It won't take me a minute.'

She half-turned but her grandmother flapped a hand to push her into a chair.

'Can't you tell when I'm kidding? Hand over one of them 'tomato sandwiches'.' This time, she mimicked Gemma's English intonation, and they smiled at each other, old and young eyes meeting in understanding before Ruth's glance flickered to Gemma's clothes. A look of anxiety came into her face.

'You've changed,' she said sharply, 'that's more than a pair of sandals you've got on.'

A green, linen shift had replaced the casual shorts and shirt, and Gemma had brushed her hair to silky smoothness, adding a touch of make-up which enhanced the deep tan she had acquired. Her grandmother's lips tightened.

'Are you going to the store? Well, I'm not having you drive down that track alone and then through all those intersections downtown. I'm coming with you.'

'You're doing nothing of the kind. I know my way now, and I'm perfectly capable. As for the track, you've been

5

going down it alone for years and so can I.'

Ruth muttered a little more, then subsided. She was beaten, and she knew it. Gemma was independent and was not to be babied.

As she clattered down the steps to the old, white, Lincoln car, she called back over her shoulder, 'I know my way to the library, and your books are already in the boot of the car.'

Ruth called back, 'You mean the trunk!' At least it gave the old lady some satisfaction to have the last word, Gemma reflected as she trundled away down the track, sending up clouds of dust.

When the sound of the engine had died away in the distance and the peace was once more restored, Ruth was unaccountably lonely. I've spent twenty years in this place, she thought, and now, for the first time, I'm lonely, for the sight and closeness of a slip of a girl.

Setting her chair into its comforting, creaking motion again, she muttered, 'I guess blood is thicker than water, just

6

as they say.' Her last thought, before sleep overcame her, was a deep satisfaction that she had put her affairs in order.

Two miles away, Gemma emerged on to the winding road into town. Nearer to the town, the quiet road became busier, and Gemma concentrated on the unfamiliar lay-out of the streets. Driving in Oregon's towns, with four lanes and wide roads, was easier, she had decided, than driving in Britain. It was also warmer. Used to chilly springs, she felt the hot glare of the sun through the windscreen, and her dress stuck to her as she got out of the car in the parking space of the supermarket.

A woman was backing out of the doors, laden with bags of groceries. She dropped one of the sacks when Gemma collided with her.

'I'm so sorry,' Gemma said. 'That was my fault.' Still apologising, she bent to help pick up a melon that had rolled away.

'It doesn't matter, I was overloaded

anyway. Hey, are you British?'

'Yes, is it so obvious?'

'Well, nobody's going to think you're from Texas!' Her newfound acquaintance giggled.

She was clearly disposed to be friendly and Gemma hesitated to move away, feeling it would be churlish. The other girl, her hands still fully occupied, blew away the fair curls from her hot forehead.

'It's hot!' she said, and then as her eyes strayed across the road, added, 'I'd really appreciate it if you'd come and have a cold drink in the deli over there. My family and I visited London recently, and I'd love to talk to you.'

'Of course, I'd be delighted.' Gemma took one of the parcels. 'Here, let me help you with those.'

'Thanks, my car's just over there,' her companion said, indicating a racy, blue sport coupé.

As they waited for their snack in the deli, the girl chatted busily. 'I promise I won't keep you for too long, but I'd really like to know what you're doing in this small town. Are you studying at the university?'

Just for a moment, Gemma felt a prickle of resentment before she told herself that it was no good objecting to the personal questions Americans asked. It was part of their friendly, open natures. As she opened her mouth to reply, the girl chattered on.

'My name's Sugar — that's not really my name, but everyone calls me Sugar. Don't ask me why! Speaking of sweets, what'll you have? I'm ordering a banana split with three flavours and two toppings.'

Gemma's eyes widened as the man behind the counter took a boat-shaped dish to the machines, filled it with enormous dollops of boysenberry, white chocolate and cheesecake, sliced a banana around it, and, finally, covered the whole confection with whipped cream and fudge.

In the next twenty minutes, Gemma's belief in the warm friendliness of the Oregonians was doubly reinforced, as Sugar not only gave her a phone number and address to call, 'Any time you feel lonely', but also invited her to dinner the next evening. 'And bring your gran, too. Jim and the little guys'll be over the moon to welcome you both. They say I never cook unless I've got company.'

'Jim?' Gemma asked tentatively.

'Yeah, Jim's my husband, and we've got two sons. We all loved London. My brother was in England for years at school and he told me I'd love it. He was right! We went everywhere, Buckingham Palace, the Tower, Westminster Abbey, everything. You name it, we saw it!'

Gemma grinned at the young, American woman. It was impossible not to like her, or to catch her infectious vitality. But, as she was driving home, she wondered, a little apprehensively, how her grandmother would react to the sudden invitation.

Her fears were not unfounded. Ruth

began grumbling the moment Gemma appeared. Unaccountably, Gemma found it difficult to begin explaining about Sugar.

Hesitantly, she began, 'I met a nice girl, a Mrs Wherry, who lives on Walnut Boulevard. She asked us — you and me — to dinner tomorrow night.'

Ruth's only response was a sniff. Clearly, she considered the idea was totally ridiculous.

Gemma continued quietly, 'I accepted.'

'Are you crazy, girl? Me? Eating with strangers? Why, you can just get straight on to that phone and tell her, whoever she is, that it's off. Right now.'

Composedly, Gemma sat on the sofa beside Ruth and spoke quietly, but resolutely. 'I'm sorry you feel like that, Grandma, but I don't think you understand. I said, I'd accepted. I hoped that you would come, too, since you were included in the invitation, but if you refuse, I shall go without you.'

There was silence. Ruth was not used

to being crossed, but she knew that in her quiet granddaughter she had met her match. She continued to bluster, and Gemma let her carry on until finally she got to her feet, saying lightly, 'Well, let's forget all about it until tomorrow. Come now, and see what I bought us for our supper. I think you'll like it.'

She held out both her hands, smiling at the older woman as though there had been no disagreement between them. Ruth, who had spent most of her life browbeating less-dominant individuals into subjection, found herself returning the smile and allowing herself to be drawn to her feet.

★   ★   ★

As Gemma got ready next evening, she was aware of Ruth sitting outside in the warmth of the spring evening, the speed of the rocker on the boards a sure indication that Grandma was not in the best of humours. Gemma, however, was not going to allow herself to be upset or to have her evening ruined. She took her time over dressing but once she was ready, went out on to the veranda and said, 'Well now, how do I look?'

'Come here.' Ruth's voice thickened with emotion and she held out imperious arms. Gemma kneeled down and hugged her grandmother.

'I promise I won't be late,' she whispered into the grey tendrils of hair at the old woman's neck. 'I've put a tray of supper in the kitchen for you.'

Ruth released her, albeit reluctantly. Testily, to hide the strength of her emotions, she grumbled, 'Get off, and stop fussing. I've managed to feed myself all these years, haven't I? Sooner you're gone, sooner you're back.'

Smiling, Gema stood up, clattered down the wooden steps and walked across the clearing to the car. Stopping only to blow a kiss to her grandmother, she stepped into the old car and turned the starter. Just before the ignition roared, she heard the tinkling of the metal chimes

13

hanging from the veranda.

Her tyres threw up gravel, dust and dirt as she jerked the big car around the bends of the track but it was no more than a few miles to Walnut Boulevard, where Sugar lived. When she arrived at the two-storey house, she drove on to the flat parking space, beside the little, blue coupé. Nimbly, she stepped out on to her unaccustomed, high heels, turned to lock the car door and twisted her foot. A cry was forced from her at the sudden, wrenching pain, and loss of balance.

She staggered and would have fallen, except for the totally unexpected grasp of the pair of strong arms which steadied and held her. Another car, even bigger and much newer, had drawn up beside hers. Its occupant, a tall, muscular, fair-haired man had reached her at the right moment to prevent a fall.

'Thanks,' Gemma gasped. 'You saved my life.'

The man smiled and said in a deep, unaccented voice. 'I think you're exaggerating a little, but at least we managed to avoid a nasty fall.'

Tall as she was, Gemma still had to look up at this lithe, Nordic-looking giant. He continued to hold her but the concerned look on his tanned face changed to one of interest.

'You're British?' he enquired.

'Yes,' Gemma assented.

'I don't suppose you're the dinner guest my sister invited me to meet?'

Gemma laughed as they turned towards the door and he pressed the bell. She said, privately wondering how this sophisticated stranger and her new friend could be related, 'If Sugar is your sister, yes, but I didn't know there was to be another guest.'

'Or you wouldn't have come?' he suggested, his mouth curling at the corners in another smile and his eyes quizzing her.

Gemma, to her annoyance, felt the colour coming into her cheeks. 'No, of course not,' she said, 'but we only met yesterday.'

There was no time to say more. The sound of the bell had apparently released a tornado inside the house. Suddenly a dog was barking, a child was crying, and voices were heard.

'Get the door, Jim.' That was Sugar.

'I can't, honey,' came a deeper voice. 'Jeremy's crashed into the wall. Eric, get the door.' This time, the voice sounded harassed.

The stranger turned to Gemma, who was looking a little taken aback by the uproar, and raised his eyebrows slightly, apparently amused. 'Don't worry,' he murmured. 'It's always like this.'

The door was drawn slowly open and a small, solemn-faced boy looked gravely up at Gemma. Then, seeing who was beside her, his reserve disappeared.

'Grant!' he cried, flinging himself bodily into his uncle's mercifully-ready arms. 'Mom didn't say you were coming.'

Gemma watched the man catch his exuberant nephew.

'Watch your manners, Superman.' he said, ruffling the boy's hair and setting him down on to the porch under the lamp. 'Can't you see the lady? How about asking her in?'

'Hi!' the boy said, suddenly shy again, giving Gemma a sidelong look.

She held out a hand saying, 'You must be Eric. Your mother has told me about you and I'm really pleased to meet you.'

Eric, who was clearly unhappy at being well-dressed, tugged at the miniscule bow-tie perched at the collar of his shirt.

'Well,' his uncle prompted, 'ask her in.'

Eric stepped aside, but had no time to say anything else before a whirlwind descended on them — his mother. 'Oh, my,' she began. 'Here you all are, still out on the porch. For goodness sake, come on in.'

She shepherded them into a large room with wooden walls and antique, pioneer-style furniture. Sugar sat them down, pushed bowls of corn chips and salsa towards them and poured sherry, before she drew breath.

'This is Grant, my brother. He lives in the woods out of town, too. Eric — get off Grant's knee.' Neither took any notice, and Sugar continued, 'Sure hope you like sherry. We bought this in London, England, but I guess it's the only European thing here tonight. I've made a Mexican dish and a boysenberry pie.

'Oh — here's Jim.'

A well-built man came down the wooden, open stairs beside another small boy — Jeremy, presumably. Gemma considered getting up, but decided against it, because she was sitting in a net chair, hanging from the beams like a sailor's hammock. She found it surprisingly comfortable and the gentle, swinging movement was soothing. 'I feel like a child in a swing, relaxed and dreamy,' she said when Sugar paused for breath.

'The chair? I got that down by the coast in an art shop,' Sugar told her.

'When they said that it would hold four hundred pounds in weight I knew it was for me.'

In the ensuing laughter, Gemma gazed through her lashes at Grant. He was, she judged, about thirty and, in spite of an easy, cosmopolitan air, exuded a maleness like the Oregon outdoors.

Although dressed in a white shirt and well-cut trousers, he looked, somehow, as though he would be more at home in a checked shirt and denims. He turned, caught her eyes, and turned away again, but not before the corners of his mouth quirked. He had caught her looking him over and was amused.

Conversation, over the excellent dinner of burritos and enchiladas, revealed that Grant was the owner of a logging firm which cut its own timber to the north of the town. It was, a business which had been in the family for many years.

'And now it's all Grant's.' Sugar laughed. 'I got my share — my dowry

— when I married Jim.'

Gemma told them that she, too, lived north of the town. As she turned back from speaking to Jim, she found Grant's eyes on hers, studying her with an intensity she found embarrassing.

'Maybe you're somewhere near my land,' Grant remarked.

Gemma felt warm. His voice was almost a caress, particularly when he said, 'My land.' Could he, she wondered, be as attracted to her as she was to him? Fervently, she hoped so, because he was surely the most interesting man she had ever met.

As she looked at them both, Sugar's eyes were bright and hopeful. She shooed the boys off to bed.

Sugar began to pour strong, black coffee and urged them to take it to the easy chairs. Gemma took hers first and settled herself on the big couch. Grant, having taken his cup from his sister, sat beside her instantly. She was suddenly a little breathless at the proximity of this attractive, masculine presence.

Sugar, sinking into the big recliner opposite them, kicked off her shoes with a sigh of relief and said engagingly, 'Don't mind, do you, Gemma? I usually live in trainers and only put these on in your honour.'

'I'll join you,' Gemma said as she leaned down and pulled off her shoes, too, curling her leg under her, acutely aware of Grant's arm laid casually behind her, across the back of the couch. It was almost touching her shoulders and she could feel an anticipatory prickle on the back of her neck.

Jim was last to take a seat and the conversation became general.

'Is that right?' Grant said in answer to a question Jim had put to him, and for the first time Gemma noticed a trace of accent. For, until now, in contrast to his sister, he had seemed to speak no differently from herself.

'Grant,' she began speaking directly to him, 'how is that you have no local accent?'

'Our parents had big ideas, gleaned from stories of the English aristocracy years ago. So I was sent to Britain to school and then taken around Europe and parts of Asia for two years. Once I'd got my forestry diploma, I'd have preferred to go back among the trees but I have to admit that it did me a lot of good.

'When our parents died, and I was suddenly in charge of the whole shoot, I guess I was more prepared than I would have been if I'd never travelled, or left Oregon.'

Just as Jim said heartily, 'Well, who'd like another drink?' the telephone rang.

With an, 'I'll get it,' Sugar picked up the receiver. After a cheery, 'Oh, hi, Doc,' her look at Gemma was anxious. Her tone had changed completely as she said, 'Oh, no, wouldn't you just know it. Don't worry, Doc, we'll bring her back. She'll be right with you.'

She replaced the receiver but by then, the others were on their feet. Sugar went quickly to Gemma, who was apprehensively gazing at her, wide-eyed, knowing that it was bad news of some kind.

'Sit down again, honey.' Sugar was biting her lip, looking at Gemma, seeming uncertain, for once, what to say.

Ignoring the suggestion to sit down, Gemma put a hand out imploringly and pleaded, 'Tell me, please, what is it?' Though Grant said nothing, she felt a strong arm come around her shoulder and hold her comfortingly.

'I'm real sorry, Gemma,' Sugar faltered. 'Seems you left my name and number back at your grandma's house. She's sick, so sick that — well, we're going to take you straight back home now. If we don't — the Doc says you may not be in time.'

'Oh, no.' Gemma gave an anguished cry of horror and buried her face in her hands. 'I didn't know.' She lifted her tear-stained face to cry out, 'I didn't know there was anything seriously wrong with her.'

'No, no, of course you didn't.' His face was filled with compassion as his deep, slow voice soothed her. He pressed the tissue that Sugar wordlessly handed to him against her cheeks. Through her crying, she could hear a hurried consultation between Grant, Jim and Sugar. Grant himself brought the discussion to a close with a firm, 'There's no problem. I'm taking her home and I'll keep you informed. Come on, Gemma. Right now.'

Gemma, by now sufficiently in control, raised her head to say, 'Thanks, but nobody need take me. I've got my own — I've got my grandmother's car.'

Grant, who was taking her jacket from Sugar and putting it round her shoulders, brushed the objection aside. 'There's no question of you driving yourself. You've had a shock. I'm taking you home and staying with you as long as you need someone. Goodbye, Sugar. I'll call you later.'

He led her relentlessly, one hand round her arm, towards the door.

Gemma would have been inside the Cadillac within the second, but she held back, determined to show some spirit. 'What about my car?' she objected.

'It'll be fine,' Grant insisted. 'Tomorrow, one of my men can drive it home for you. Come on, Gemma.' His voice was insistent. 'I hate to remind you, but we can't ignore what the doctor said about hurrying. I want to get you back in time.'

Gemma's resistance collapsed, but before she got into the car she turned quickly to Sugar and gave her a convulsive hug. 'You've been so good. I'm sorry to have spoiled the party, but very glad we've met.'

Sugar hugged her back, sympathy written all over her face. 'Go now. We'll get together real soon.'

Grant backed the car out of the drive and turned into Jefferson Avenue. Jim and Sugar waved until the car turned a corner and was lost to sight.

Gemma said contritely, 'They've been so kind. I wouldn't have ruined their evening like this — yours too — for anything else.'

A passing headlight lit up Grant's face and she saw his wry smile.

'You haven't ruined it,' he said. 'Far from it. None of this is your fault. It's just one of those things.'

A red traffic light gleamed high above the road in front of them and Grant drew the purring car to a halt. 'I've headed north of the town,' he said, 'but you'll have to direct me from here.'

'Of course, I forgot you didn't know the way.' Gemma sat upright and prepared to put aside her worry for the moment.

'If you go right out on this same road for three miles, you'll see a little turning into a place called Markham's Creek. Turn there — it's only a dirt road — and our place is about two miles into the forest.'

Because she was looking straight ahead as she spoke, she missed the sudden, startled look he gave her, but she gasped and held on to the side of the car as she swung across the wide, front seat. Only her seat belt prevented her from sliding into Grant.

'I'm sorry.' His voice was clipped. Was it her imagination, Gemma wondered, or had he become, in some mysterious way, cold towards her. The little cocoon of intimacy was either removed, or had never been there in the first place.

'I swerved, I'm afraid.' Then, as an afterthought, he asked, 'Are you quite sure you're all right?'

In a low voice, she assured him she was, and neither spoke until the lights picked up the sign 'Markham's Creek'. There was one, solitary mailbox standing at the turn, with the name 'Lawrence' in faded, white paint.

Somehow, the atmosphere in the car had been altered since the swerve. Without understanding why, Gemma felt a different aura coming from her companion. She half-wished Jim had brought her home, because in some inexplicable way, Grant was no longer comfortable to be with.

As they scrunched into sight of the cabin, he drew up with a jerk and she saw two other cars parked in the clearing. One she recognised as belonging to Matt Fulton, who was a neighbour, friend and occasional employee of her grandmother. The other belonged to the doctor.

Grant leaned across her and opened the door on her side. As she undid her seat belt and made to get out, he detained her.

'Gemma?'

'Yes?' She was impatient to go to her grandmother, and the grim look on his face was daunting. It was no longer the seriousness of compassion, but was something else, something frightening.

'I'm going now. I know that I said I'd stay but . . . ' he gestured towards the cars. 'You have other people to support you.'

'Of course.' Gemma tried to hide her disappointment, and hurt. 'Thank you for everything,' she called, but he had already started the engine and did not hear her. Even as she turned and hurried towards the steps to face whatever awaited her indoors, the tail lights of his sleek vehicle were disappearing down the track.

2

'I'm all right, truly I am.'

Gemma worked hard at maintaining a calm manner on the transatlantic telephone line. The last thing she wanted was to worry her mother. The truth was that she felt lonely, grief-stricken and scared, so when the call had come she had gone out of her way to allay her mother's anxieties.

'How did the funeral go?' her mother was asking. 'Did someone help you with the arrangements?'

'Yes, it went as well as such things can. I had the doctor, Grandma's lawyer and a neighbour, a Mr Fulton, to help.'

Into her head, yet again, popped the question, 'Why hadn't Grant come?'

The morning after the dinner party, the old car had been delivered by two men, plainly loggers. They had brought her the keys, been thanked, said, 'Our pleasure, ma'am' and driven away. Gemma had still been in a state of shock but had felt confident that Grant would get in touch with her.

Angrily, she thought, how could he be so heartless? What had she done to upset him? She was especially hurt by not having heard from Sugar. The family had been so kind that night, that suddenly to have dropped her like this, at such a dreadful period, was incredible. The death announcement had appeared in the local paper so she was sure that they knew.

Her mother was asking, 'And it's true, is it, that she left you everything?'

Gemma shifted uncomfortably in the chair. 'Yes, it's true but I expect it's just the house and the piece of land round it. I feel guilty about it.'

'There's no reason why you should.' Her mother was soothing. 'You were her only living relative. I wish you had been able to meet her when you were younger, but at least you had some time together.'

'I know.' Gemma was suddenly overcome with a desire to cry and knew that she couldn't keep up a brave face much longer. Quickly, she said, 'I'll write you a long airmail today, I promise, and tell you everything you want to know, but this call must be costing you a fortune.'

'All right, Gemma, I'll ring off. Take care — and promise you'll call immediately if you need me,' her mother finished by saying.

Gemma crossed her fingers and promised. Shakily, she put the phone down. She padded out to the veranda, looking up at the waving firs. The warm air felt good to her skin but the silence was oppressive.

Sighing, Gemma lifted the rug from the rocker, sat down and with one bare foot, began to push herself to and fro. She smiled sadly to herself, seeming to hear the admonitory voice — 'Get some shoes on!' She lifted the rug to her face and laid her cheek against it. Then, tucking it behind her head, she gazed upwards to the little patch of blue sky showing between the tall firs.

She wondered again, what her grandmother had meant by her words on that awful last night, when Gemma had returned just in time to find the old lady still conscious. With Matt Fulton and the doctor watching her sympathetically, she had kneeled, distraught, beside the bed and clasped the wrinkled hands between her two warm ones.

Ruth had opened her eyes and smiled weakly as Gemma murmured, 'Grandma, I'm here. Oh, I'm so sorry I wasn't here before.'

Behind her, the doctor had whispered to Mr Fulton, 'Guess she was just hanging on until the girl got here.'

Ruth's eyes had still been intelligent as she tried to speak, but her voice was no more than a reedy breath of air. Gemma, holding back her tears, leaned close to hear what her grandmother was trying to say.

'Doesn't matter, honey, you're here now.' The old lady had sighed as though content, closed her eyes again and, for a moment or two, there had been no sound in the room. Then, gazing at Gemma's face, she opened her mouth to speak, struggling hard to communicate. 'Listen, Gemma, listen. When I'm gone, you take care. Those Markhams. They'll try — you take care — don't sell!'

Gemma had wanted to ask what she meant but her grandmother had made her last effort. Her head dropped sideways on the pillow, her eyes closed again, this time for good, and a weeping Gemma had been shepherded from the bedroom by the two men.

Matt Fulton's arms held her comfortingly, if a little awkwardly, in the first outburst of her grief. Even then, she wished they could have been the arms of the man she had met earlier that night.

The creaking of the chair on the boards slowed and stilled as Gemma's tiredness took its toll and she fell asleep against the softness of the rug behind her head. How long she slept, she didn't know, but the peace was shattered by the insistent sound of the telephone. Coming swiftly to her feet and dashing indoors, she wondered if it could be her mother again.

The voice on the other end of the phone, unmistakably Grant's, was a heart-stopping surprise.

For a moment, still confused, she did not know how to reply to his cool, 'Gemma? I'm really sorry about your grandmother. We saw the announcement in the paper.'

Gemma, pulling herself together, was determined to match his coolness. Lightly, distantly, she said, 'I'm fine, thanks.'

After the pause which followed, he finally said, seemingly with some diffidence, 'I should like to see you again. Would you have dinner with me in town?'

No explanations, Gemma thought,

no excusing, 'I've been out of town,' just, 'Here I am again.'

He had said nothing in the nature of an apology or a word of real compassion.

She was sorely tempted to refuse. Hot words tumbled to her lips but she bit them back. She had wanted to see him again, hadn't she? Anyway, she had been dreading another long evening alone in the house in the forest. So, keeping her voice steady, she asked, 'Do you mean tonight?'

'Yes. I'm sorry it's such short notice. Can you make it?'

How formal his manner was! It was hard to equate this stranger with the friendly, warm man of the evening at his sister's house. What a long time ago that seemed! Gemma answered deliberately, 'Yes, I think I should like that. Since my grandmother's death, I've not left this house, except for the funeral.'

'It must have been hard for you. I'm glad you can come. Is seven o'clock a good time?'

'Seven will be fine.' Gemma wasn't going to say anything to dispel the awkwardness between them

Grant became brisk and practical.

'I'll make a reservation at the Depot, then. It's a converted train station and the food is good. It's by the river so there's plenty to look at. I'll come by to pick you up.'

'Thank you.'

Gemma wondered how long she could keep up these clipped monosyllables, but she didn't have long to worry about that because he simply said, 'See you then,' and hung up.

After replacing the receiver, Gemma wondered whether she had been foolish to accept the dinner invitation. Still, it was exciting to be going out again. If it was even more exciting to be seeing Grant again, she was still too hurt and angry by this and Sugar's silence to dwell on that.

Quickly, she rifled through the few clothes she'd brought from home. Nothing seemed just right. Finally, she chose a deep, blue dress. The neckline was cut low and her big earrings reflected the colour. Once she had bathed and dressed, she felt more like herself than she had for weeks. For too long, she thought, she had been alone and had worn only shirts and shorts.

Fifteen minutes later, she was ready. Slipping into high-heeled sandals, she went out on to the wooden veranda to enjoy the early evening of the forest, where a pink-hued light spread magical shafts down through the trees.

She was startled by the sight of a figure just below. It was Matt Fulton. He was standing utterly still, looking up at her as if he'd never seen her before.

Unaware of how stunning she looked, she said casually, 'Hi, Matt.' For some reason, she felt uncomfortable but the moment soon passed as she offered him a drink and went indoors to fetch a beer from the fridge.

When she returned, he was sitting on the rail, very much at ease, one booted foot swinging, his back against the support post. He thanked her for the drink but waved away the glass, snapping open the top and drinking straight from the can.

She wondered why he had called but decided that it was probably just a friendly gesture. Matt had always been around a lot. He had been the only person her grandmother had tolerated and had chopped wood, cleared brush and done other heavy work for her.

Sometimes, after Gemma had gone to bed, she had heard them conversing easily and laughing together. He was in his early forties, unmarried and living alone, apparently enjoying his free and easy life. Now he said, 'Just got to wondering how you were managing up here, all alone. I thought maybe there'd be something else I could do for you — besides checking your mailbox every day.'

'Have you been doing that, Matt? Thank you. That was nice of you. But there's really nothing else. It's good to know that I can walk down to your place if I do want something.'

Being sublimely unaware of how entrancing she looked as she smiled up at him, she could not guess the reason for the renewed edginess in the man's attitude.

'Thought any more about what you're going to do?' Matt asked.

'To do? Oh, you mean about the property?' Gemma's smile died. For the first time, the unwelcome thought occurred to her that perhaps Matt Fulton had had expectations before she came upon the scene.

'I don't really know exactly what I own yet. It's probably just the house and the bit of land around it. The lawyer is dealing with it all.'

Matt turned and looked out at the trees, bathed in shafts of evening light. He took his time replying as though to measure his words. 'Lot more to it than that. Ruth's land ain't just the bit you see here. She's got at least a hundred acres of old-growth fir, left from an early land grant. It's not been cut and

40

the old lady wouldn't sell. Guess the Markhams used every trick in the book to get it off her, including letting her name any price she wanted. She didn't tell you that?'

Gemma's face showed her astonishment. Her eyes wide, her lips lightly parted, she gazed at him incredulously. 'No, she didn't tell me any of that. I had no idea. But I know that she loved this place and certainly wouldn't have wanted to sell it.'

'Loved!' Matt seemed to try the word out for size before rejecting it. 'Loved is nothing compared to how she felt about her land, and her trees. She'd sooner lose her life than lose her land.'

There was an uncomfortable silence as he realised what he had said. He got up, still looking out at the forest, and mumbled, 'I'm real sorry. I shouldn't have said that.'

At Gemma's dismissive little gesture of acceptance, he continued in a voice filled with anger.

'She was forced to sell little bits off,

though. Bits round the edge. No other way she could carry on living here. And I'm telling you she hated them for that and she said sometimes they were closing in on her.'

Gemma's eyes were damp. She lifted a finger to wipe away a tear. It seemed that, along with her illness, her grandmother had lived with the fear of losing her beloved home. Whoever the Markhams were, she vowed, she too would hate them for what they had done to make the last few years of her grandmother's life miserable.

After a moment she said quietly, 'Grandma's last words to me were something like that. Who are the Markhams?'

'Biggest operation in this area.' Matt continued to look out at the trees instead of at her. 'Gobbled up a whole heap of smaller landowners. Most of the big, logging trucks you see going by are theirs.'

'Oh.' Gemma digested this information. 'But if they're such a big business, they must have a lot of land. Why are they so anxious to have this place?'

'Beats me.' Matt was a man of few words but as Gemma waited he volunteered, 'Maybe 'cos it's a fine piece, with good growth, slap bang in the middle of theirs. They could cut a path to the road along here and save themselves a few miles.'

'Is that all? For that they'd harass a sick, old woman?'

'Harass. Yeah.' Matt's voice was full of brooding fury. 'She felt like they were her mortal enemies, it was a real feud.'

Gemma wanted to ask for more details but, at the moment, she became aware of the arrival of a car. Rising to her feet, she missed the look on Matt's face as he saw it drive into the clearing.

Slightly ashamed of her excitement she said, 'I'm afraid I'm going to have to leave you now, Matt. I'm going out for the evening. Thanks for coming.'

'My pleasure,' he replied, but he did not move. His eyes were fixed on Grant, who had got out of the car and was walking, loose-limbed, towards the steps.

He was, Gemma saw, looking as handsome as she remembered, in a crisp, white shirt and jeans and a denim jacket.

In two or three easy strides, he had reached the steps and stood looking up at Matt. There was no smile on either face. Though Grant carried none of the weight of the older man, he was as tall.

They nodded curtly at each other in apparently reluctant acknowledgement, before Grant turned, for the first time, to look at Gemma. His eyes swept down over her, from his gleaming hair to her high-heeled, blue sandals. He smiled, an intimate smile, a spontaneous smile; a smile that arose simply from pleasure at the picture she made. But, in spite of what his eyes were saying, he merely asked if she were ready.

'Yes, quite ready.' She turned to the silent figure of the other man and extended her hand. 'Goodbye, Matt.

Please do call again.'

He simply nodded, without speaking.

Grant drove fast around the bends to the road and she was acutely aware of his closeness and maleness.

He said nothing until they came out on the main road and then he began, 'That man, Matt Fulton. Does he come around much? Does he bother you at all?'

Gemma was suprised and a little resentful. 'He's been kind and Grandma liked him. He often worked for her and she said she wouldn't have been able to manage without his help. I didn't know you knew him.'

'Oh, yes, I know him.'

His voice held a trace of something suspiciously like contempt. Gemma wondered why and asked, 'Don't you like him? If you've any reason to distrust him, I think I should be told. He's the only person who's visited my grandmother — and I'm all alone out there, now.'

'It's true that I don't like him.' Grant

was frowning. 'But I have to be honest and say that it's an instinctive dislike. He worked for my firm for a while, but that was years ago, when my father was still alive. I've only met him a few times, since I've been back. Unfortunately, none of those meetings was particularly friendly.'

A thought occurred to Gemma. 'Did you know my grandmother?' she asked eagerly.

Grant stared straight ahead. His voice was deliberately even as he replied, 'I'd seen her in town. I knew her by sight.'

Gemma was sure she could not be mistaken — there was definitely a strange note in his voice. She disliked mysteries and would have asked further questions but they had drawn up at the restaurant, which was a long, low building surrounded by masses of flowers on each side of the door.

Although The Depot was a converted railway station, the old line must have run close to the water for, inside, all the luxuriously-appointed booths boasted river views. Grant was obviously well-known and his custom valued for they were ushered straight to a corner booth with a view of a willow tree overhanging the wide, Willamette River.

As Gemma sat down she caught sight of ducks swimming busily by, almost beneath the window.

Grant sat down opposite her.

When the waitress had handed them the wine list and menu, Gemma leaned forward and said, 'It's lovely, Grant. Thank you for bringing me here.' She noticed that his answering grin reached clear to his eyes, which crinkled at the corners. He must smile a lot, she thought, inconsequently.

The business of choosing dinner was fun. Grant recommended an Oregon wine that, he said came from a vineyard which belonged to a friend of his. Later, when it came, she pronounced it delightful — light and fruity. As their eyes met over the wine glasses, his were warmly approving.

Although her mind was still full of questions, she had no wish to spoil the growing magic of the evening. For over a week now, grief and loneliness had been her lot; just for a few hours, she meant to put them behind her. Clearly, Grant was anxious to help her forget her troubles.

As they finished their meal with 'coffee nudges' — concoctions of coffee, brandy and cream — she wondered if, perhaps, she were a little light-headed. Could this kind of rapport, this electricity between two people, be possible on such a short acquaintance? His voice, when he spoke to her, was no less than a caress. Even when they rose to leave, the touch of his hand under her bare elbow made her feel warm.

Grant stopped at the desk to pay the bill and Gemma asked for the ladies' cloakroom. 'Rest-room's just round the corner,' was the reply.

As Gemma turned to go in the direction indicated, the girl looked up at Grant, who was holding out his credit card and said, 'It's real nice to see you here, Mr Markham. We don't see you too often.'

It was only the momentum of her movements that kept Gemma walking on. Somehow, she resisted the sudden inclination to cry out, 'Markham? Your name is Markham?'

As it was, she turned, as she pushed the swing door, and gave him a searing look. He, too, was looking at her and his eyes contained an uncharacteristic 'small boy found out' expression.

They had been gazing at each other all evening, but now they were looking at each other like two combatants. Momentarily, Grant had lost all his poise but that was all Gemma had time to note before she was through the door.

Later, inside, as she looked at herself in the mirror, she saw that her face had whitened under its tan and her eyes were huge with shock. As she took a comb and lipstick out of her handbag, her hands were shaking.

It was a different Gemma who emerged into the reception area to meet her escort, a brittle, angry, girl. As he held open the door for her to pass through into the black, diamond-studded night, she said in a clear, deliberate voice, 'Thank you, Mr Markham.'

In the light of the lamp, outside the door, she could see his face and he looked back at her with an equally-hard look but he said nothing until they were side by side in his car. Then, making no attempt to switch on the ignition, he turned his body sideways and said in his deep, level voice, 'I guess someone has been talking — and the name Markham means something to you.'

Before he could say more, Gemma burst out, speaking quickly and intensely, 'Yes, it does. Until tonight, I wondered why you hadn't been in touch with me after — after your friendliness. Now, I do know. You're the family — the owner — of the firm that made my grandmother's last years miserable, aren't you?

Grant said drily, 'I am, but I'd quarrel with that interpretation. Was Matt Fulton your informant, by any chance?'

'Yes, he was.' Gemma was flushed with fury. 'But it doesn't matter who told me, for someone would have, eventually. Did you expect to get away with it, without my finding out?'

He leaned forward and turned the ignition key and the engine roared into activity. As he swung the Cadillac out of the parking space on to the wide road, he said, in a voice full of supressed anger, 'What do you mean by 'getting away with it'?'

'You know perfectly well what I mean.' Gemma, who, whilst never a submissive person, had always disliked rows, was painfully aware of how easily her tears could rise to the surface.

She struggled hard to remain in command of herself and swept on, 'You changed your attitude to me the

51

moment you discovered who I was at the end of that first evening. I imagine that both you and Sugar decided to have nothing more to do with me, even though you both knew that I was having a hard time and was alone in a foreign country.'

'All right, all right, I'm sorry about that.' Grant did not look at her as he said it but concentrated on his driving. 'I felt that nothing but trouble could come of our getting to know each other too well. And don't blame Sugar — I talked her into staying away, too.'

'Oh, thanks.' Gemma was bitter. Boiling resentment rose within her. 'Just when I needed a friend! And why the sudden change — as though I didn't know.

'Then, out of the blue, you ring me, arranged a date and become so — so friendly. This evening couldn't have been nicer. You certainly know how to please a woman, don't you — until she realises you have ulterior motives?

'All the time, you were hoping either

that I wouldn't find out your name, or that I wouldn't understand what the name Markham meant to my grand-mother — and therefore to me.'

If she had expected him to rush into a defensive speech, she was disap-pointed. Instead, he was silent for a moment, then gave a deep sigh. Looking straight ahead, over the steer-ing wheel, he said, rather slowly, 'If that's what you mean by 'getting away with it', then I suppose I shall have to plead guilty. I did hope that my name meant nothing to you but that was because I didn't want you prejudiced against me.

'Surely you can understand that? You must have known I was attracted to you.'

Gemma was suddenly breathless; left, for the moment, with nothing to say. She had felt that he was drawn to her and she had most certainly felt similarly drawn to him on their first meeting.

He turned and looked at her, although it was hard to read his expression in the dim light of the street lamps. They had come close to the end of the road and the car swerved as it turned onto the dirt track.

Gemma said sharply, 'I suggest you pay more attention to your driving.'

Unexpectedly, Grant laughed out loud and the sound broke the tension between them.

'Don't be such a shrew,' he said in his normal, lazy voice, and then, more soberly, 'but we do have to sort this out. May I come in and talk with you? Surely I deserve a fair hearing!'

'I was going to ask you in, anyway.'

Nothing further was said until he had drawn up in the clearing, where the house sat darkly, dwarfed by the fir trees. Later, Gemma was to wonder why she had been so ready to invite him into the lonely house, but no thought of danger ever crossed her mind. Whatever the feud between his family and hers, she instinctively felt that he was to be trusted.

She had forgotten to leave the porch

light on and he brushed against her as they felt their way up the wooden steps. Sensing her hesitation, Grant said, 'I was a fool not to leave the headlights on. Shall I go back?'

'No, really, we're almost in.' As she spoke, Gemma almost tumbled over the top step.

At once, strong arms were around her and he said, 'Is this a repeat performance?' Too flustered for a moment to recall their first meeting, she blushed, and was glad the darkness hid her embarrassment.

Stepping forward, she unlocked and pulled back the door on the veranda. She clicked on the inside switch and both of them were bathed in soft light. She saw that he was looking right at her, his expression serious.

Wanting to break the tension, she said quickly, 'Please come in,' leading the way as she spoke. 'Would you like coffee — or wine?'

'Neither. Frankly, I'd rather just sit and talk and try to clear up a few misunderstandings.'

'All right.' Gemma prepared to speak her mind. For some reason, it was much harder putting her angry thoughts into words while she was facing him. She was sure that Grant was aware of her discomfort.

After a moment, he said, 'Well?' The tone was arrogant. He had been accused and was clearly in no mood to help her out.

'I've told you already what I believe,' she said. 'I really don't have much knowledge of all this family feud stuff, but when I heard about my poor grandmother being made miserable in her last years, I hated you.'

His reply was icy. 'It doesn't really matter how you felt about me. All this 'instant hatred' is because you have listened to one person and decided that I'm a villain. Do you want to hear the truth, or don't you?'

'The truth — or your version of it?'

Her rising emotion seemed to calm him a little as he replied, 'The truth is always subjective. I can only tell you the truth, as I see it.'

Gemma was too honest to deny that and she said, a little mollified, 'Yes, I agree, but let me hear it.'

Restlessly, he rose to his feet and said, in a lighter tone, 'Could I change my mind about that coffee?'

'Of course.' Gemma, too, rose and went to the other end of the big room to switch on the coffee. Her movements were steady, although she was aware that his eyes were following her. As she came back and faced him, he reached for her in a sudden movement. She had not expected it and, as she felt herself in his arms, she gave a gasp of surprise. Before she could protest, his mouth came down on hers.

Moments later, just as abruptly as he had reached for her, he let her go again. Because the whole thing had happened so swiftly and she had not been expecting it, Gemma almost fell. Wildly, she struck at his supporting arm. She almost slapped his face in her fury but felt that such a gesture would seem foolish and melodramatic.

He knew what she was thinking and said softly, 'Don't. I might just do it back.'

Finding her voice, she cried, 'Is that why you asked me to let you in? Is this your way of trying to get my land?'

The silence in the room was broken only by the bubbling of the coffee machine. Grant had stepped back a pace, his face furious. 'So that's what you think?' His mouth was a hard line. Was that the same mouth that had pressed against her so passionately only moments ago?

'Your land! How easily that came to you!' he said bitterly. 'You sounded like your grandmother.'

'If I did, then I'm proud of it,' Gemma flung at him. 'And I'd like you to leave my land. Now!'

'Don't worry, I'm going.'

He made no move to walk away. Still they faced each other, both breathing shallowly as though they had been running. The bubbling of the coffee machine had stopped and from the outside came the mournful cry of an owl.

As he looked at her, his face softened and he made a slight movement towards her. 'Gemma?'

'Get out!' she shouted, and turned away from his half-extended arm.

For a moment, there was no sound and she wondered, apprehensively, whether he would try once more to take her in his arms. Then she heard him stride towards the door to the veranda and step out. Only when it slid back, did she turn to look after him, seeing his wide shoulders disappearing into the darkness.

A wild desire to call him back was followed by an equally-strong wish to burst into tears. She gave way to neither. Firmly, she forced herself to walk steadily into the kitchenette, unplug the coffee machine, turn off the light and climb the open, wooden stairs to her gallery bedroom.

3

As yet, Gemma had not used the bedroom which had been her grandmother's. Tonight, still smarting from the recent scene, she opened the door and looked at the big, double bed, with its patchwork quilt folded neatly across the bottom.

Saying 'my land' had crystallised something in her head that, until now, she had been unwilling to acknowledge. Finally, she was ready to step into her grandmother's shoes; this was her place. Smiling a little, she went forward, switched on the old-fashioned, bedside lamp and turned back the white sheets.

From now on, this would be her room. This would be her home — and no-one had the right to take it away from her!

A moment later, she got into the big bed and heard a muffled creak from her previous room. For a moment of stark terror, she remained absolutely still, but then her brain began to rationalise. The old boards were bound to move. How many nights had she lain in that very room and heard sounds all around?

Once, it had been a deer stepping across the veranda, once, chipmonks had scurried across the wooden railing, opossums had snuffed about. There was a reasonable explanation, she told herself. But she was wrong . . .

The sudden shrilling of the telephone startled her. Quickly, she threw back the sheets and hurried across the room and down the stairs, switching on lights as she went.

She picked up the receiver and said, 'Hello?'

'Gemma?' The deep, questioning voice was unmistakably that of the man who had left her no more than half an hour ago.

'Gemma, I'm sorry. I shouldn't have stormed out. We didn't talk about anything that matters.'

Gemma was still silent and he said anxiously, 'Gemma, are you listening?'

'Yes.' It was a small word, and quiet, but it seemed to reassure him.

He began again. 'Look, darling, it's not our quarrel, not really. Please, give me another chance.'

Gemma heard the endearment and felt her head swimming. 'Darling!' How easily he dropped it into the conversation. When she spoke, she was cool. 'I don't know what you mean by 'another chance.' You could have said anything you wanted to say, tonight, if you hadn't grabbed me.'

'If you didn't want to be 'grabbed' you shouldn't look so enchanting.'

Suddenly, she wanted to speak of her fears. 'When you left,' she said haltingly, 'I was frightened.'

'What?' His voice was sharp. 'Frightened by what?'

'I thought someone was watching me, up in the bedroom. I thought I heard a noise.'

Just the fact that she had said it,

shared it with someone else, made Gemma lose some of her fears.

'It's nothing but my imagination,' she hurried on. 'Of course, there's no-one here. I've got worked up about hearing things before, and I must just overcome it.'

'Will you be all right? Would you like me to come?'

Gemma said provocatively, 'So that you can grab me again? That would be real danger as opposed to imaginary danger.'

Grant laughed. 'Maybe you're right. I couldn't guarantee that I could resist all temptation. But if anything worries you, ring me and I'll be over within minutes. Promise me you'll do that.'

Gemma promised, feeling warm and protected.

'Look, I'm sure it's bad for you to be there, alone so much. I've got a house on the beach. Come for the week-end and have a break.'

'Are you mad?' she gasped indignantly. 'Do you honestly think I'd come away with you for the week-end?'

'Listen to me. I really do mean that it would be a relaxing week-end. If you like, I'll drive you there and leave you until it's time to bring you back but I think it would be better for you to have company.'

Gemma's second refusal was less vehement. Grant was persuasive. By the time she put the 'phone down, she had allowed him to talk her into going with him to his house on the coast. He promised to look after her, like any good friend.

Once back in bed, she was too full of the coming trip to remember her previous fears. She fell asleep on the hazy thought that, had he not phoned her, she might have suspected him of parking the car down the track and coming back to spy on her. Could she really trust her instincts where he was concerned?

★   ★   ★

In the bright, morning sunshine, her fears of the night seemed fanciful. As she sat out on the veranda with a cup of coffee, she made a list of things she wanted to buy in town, in order to set her personal mark on her surroundings.

Feeling like a pioneer woman, she bought all she needed for her 'homestead.' Later, back at the cabin, she set to work. She dug around the base of the steps and veranda, as much as she could, but it was harder work than she had anticipated. By late evening, she had many small patches of earth with tiny pansies and begonias, hopefully standing to attention. Three flower-filled baskets hanging over the deck railings made a nice change from the set of chimes that tinkled in the air. Ruefully, she groaned as she straightened up, promising herself a long, hot bath at the end of the day.

From that day on, Gemma discovered in herself a violent desire to get to grips with making her inheritance 'hers'. She cleaned, swept, climbed impossible heights to reach cobwebs, cleared out cupboards, polished old brass hinges, washed every piece of linen she could find and gloried in the emergence of her house as a cosy nest.

On Thursday, the day Grant was coming to take her to the coast, she had again had a miserable night. She began to feel that she was Ruth, the young Ruth, the Ruth who must have grieved over the death of her husband and, then, her son, with no-one to comfort her.

She found herself sobbing into the darkness of the bedroom. Oh, Ruth, if only I had known you before. We had such a short time together, she thought.

So, if Grant expected a lively companion, he was doomed to disappointment. It was a heavy-eyed Gemma who met him at the base of the steps, although she tried to smile. He took her lightweight bag and tossed it into the back of the car, looking keenly into her face. Then he took her chin between two fingers.

Gemma, feeling herself scrutinised, twisted her head but he imprisoned it saying, 'You look as if you've had a bad time.'

'Thanks,' she said lightly. 'Are you telling me I look a mess?'

'No.' He opened the car door for her. 'I'm certainly not that foolhardy — but something's been bugging you. Are you going to tell me what it is?'

Gemma thought that he was the last person with whom she could share her regret over the loss of her grandmother. Paradoxically, the sight of this tall, handsome, arrogant man had reawakened her anger and her doubts.

As he started the car, she simply replied, in a cool voice, 'No, actually, I'm not going to tell you anything.' She left it at that.

He was clearly puzzled, but after a glance at her solemn expression, made no more enquiries but simply drove on.

The coast highway was new to Gemma, but for the first few miles, she found it hard to forget her unhappiness.

It was impossible, though, not to be aware of the scenery, the majestic hills and tree-clad slopes, but she made no comment on anything that they passed, even keeping her eyes stubbornly ahead when he pointed out particular beauty spots to her. After a few abortive efforts at conversation, he again lapsed into silence.

Eventually, he drew the car in beside a huge, flat, field of corn plants. As the engine died, Gemma looked at him enquiringly and a little apprehensively. He looked steadily back at her, his face kind but with a decisive air about him.

'You're going to have to let go of it, Gemma,' he said, putting a large, tanned hand over hers.

'Let go of what?' She was defiant, although she knew what he meant.

Grant turned back to his steering wheel, hesitated before replying, looked ahead for a moment and then swung round to her again. His voice was firm.

'You know what I'm getting at. Let go of your grief — for your own sake.

No, don't snap at me . . . ' he said as Gemma raised her chin and made as if to speak. 'You loved your grandmother — and she loved you. You've told me as much. Because of that, you can't let her death, which was inevitable, colour the rest of your life.'

'The rest of my life!' Gemma gasped furiously. 'It's been just three weeks. Is that the rest of my life?'

He smiled. 'Good. No, of course it's not, but at least you're showing some spirit now. You looked apathetic before, nothing like the girl I first met, who took so much pleasure and enjoyment from her adoptive country. I just wanted to see her face again.'

He had started the car again as he spoke and glided smoothly back on to the road. As they passed a wooden barn on the left and went into the curve of a hill, he turned his head and smiled. 'See it, Gemma. See the beauty. Don't miss it.'

Gemma looked up and around her. He was forcing her to think in a way she would rather not. Some of the talks she had had with Ruth came back to her. There had been a different note in the hard, old woman's voice when she had spoken of the woods and forest of Oregon.

'No,' Gemma said softly but with sudden certainty, 'Grandma wouldn't want me to stop appreciating this place. You're right.'

His answering laugh was compassionate and understanding until he glanced at her and saw that tears were running down her face. He apologised. 'I'm sorry. I'd no business — '

'Please, don't be sorry,' Gemma managed to say. 'Just let me cry — I'll be better afterwards. Honestly.'

After navigating a bend, he once more drew the car off the road. By now, Gemma's sobs were shaking her whole body and her face was buried in her hands.

'Here,' he said, sliding across and putting one arm round her. 'There now, cry as much as you want to.'

Gemma, finding the big, solid, shoulder conveniently to hand, leaned her head back against it and had her cry out.

He stroked her hair with his other hand, murmuring endearments and soothing words. Gemma, feeling herself securely hugged and cuddled, said a number of semi-incoherent things and was much comforted by an occasional, 'Of course you do,' or 'Don't you worry about a thing.'

Shortly, tears changed to laughter and she raised her wet face. 'You haven't any idea of what I've been talking about, have you?'

He grinned, mock-contritely. 'Well, no, I guess I haven't — but I sure feel for your distress.'

Carefully, he lifted his arm away from her and restarted the car.

After a few more miles, Gemma said suddenly, 'Don't you sometimes feel as though the trees would march right across the road if we didn't hold them back?'

Grant smiled but his reply was serious.

'Maybe they're guarding their rights, because if we don't take care of our trees we could erase them from the face of the earth. Look up there.' He pointed at a raw clearing on the hillside, covered in stumps. 'At one time, unscrupulous logging firms cut indiscriminately. Thank goodness it's been stopped.'

As he talked, Gemma watched his face grow animated. He really does love the trees and the land, she thought, as he continued to point out landmarks and hills.

They soon came within sight of the Pacific, at Lincoln City. Grant negotiated the main drag with its motels and garish signs.

As they travelled south, she saw sandy beaches and breakers crashing in on their right. The highway circled a bay where, Grant had told her, he had often caught clams.

'Crabs, too, on the mud flats,' he

said, growing reminiscent. 'When Sugar and I were kids, our dad used to bring us here. We'd make a driftwood fire at night on the beach and Mom would bring her guitar and we'd sing.'

Gemma watched his face and saw it soften with pain. Her own sorrow making her perceptive, she said, 'Every time you mention your parents it makes you sad.'

Grant did not speak for a while but eventually he volunteered, 'It's a pretty awful story. Both of them were killed outright in an out-of-state accident — returning from a trip. I came back to this country too late.'

He had eased the car down to a crawl as they passed fountains of spray.

'Those are water-spouts,' Grant informed her. 'Tomorrow, when we've rested, I'll take you to Devil's Punch Bowl and Whale Cove. Right now, we'd better push on.'

Gemma acquiesced, although she had a momentary uneasiness. Was she really wise to trust a man who was such a comparative stranger?

As though he read her thoughts, he turned to look at her, and her uneasiness deepened. Their glances locked for a few seconds. Gemma was relieved when he said in a perfectly normal voice. 'Let's just go on now and eat out later.'

After a few more miles, they turned a curve into a sandy bay, with trees behind and a stretch of driftwood-strewn beach in front. On the solid part of the dunes stood a square, wooden house on stilts.

Without a word, Grant turned the car on to the path which led to the house and drew up, virtually beneath it.

'Hope you don't mind climbing steps,' he said with a grin.

In her imagination, even when he had said a 'beach house' she had not imagined a house so truly on the beach as this one was.

'Does the tide come right up under the house?' she asked as they climbed the stairs to the wooden deck which surrounded the house.

'Not quite.' He laughed. 'But if I come here on a winter's night, when a storm is up, it feels a mite too close.'

He had dropped the bags to put the key in the door and now stood back to let her pass inside first. As she did so she cried enthusiastically, 'Grant, it's beautiful. You could stand here and watch the waves for ever.'

'Do you like it?' He sounded anxious for her approval.

'Like it? I love it!' Gemma moved towards the glass, patio doors that faced the ocean. Except for the thick carpet and the wood stove, the room held only two plumply-padded couches, separated by a big, marble coffee table.

Everything looked new and Grant explained that he had drawn the plans himself and that the house had been built only a year before. 'Although,' he added, 'the piece of land was acquired by my father a long time ago.'

Suddenly, that phrase 'piece of land

75

acquired by my father' hung in the air between them.

He broke it by asking, 'Would you like to see your bedroom and bathroom?'

Gemma assumed a nonchalance she did not feel. 'My bathroom,' she said, raising her eyebrows. 'Are there two bathrooms?'

'But of course.' Grant looked surprised. 'When my nephews come down, believe me, I'd much rather they had their own bathroom. Have you tried to shower, or bath, with two small boys climbing all over you?'

'Actually,' Gemma countered with a grin, 'I have. Often! Remember, I have two, little half-brothers.'

They had reached the left-hand bedroom and Grant threw open the door to reveal a room with two queen-sized beds and filmy, pale-green curtains — or drapes, to Americans. The effect was that of an underwater cave.

'Good gracious!' Gemma blinked.

'It's not a bit the way I expected a beach house bedroom to look.'

'This is the room I let Sugar have her head over. Believe me, the other one isn't at all like it.' He opened the door of the room on the other side of the corridor and the contrast was total. Though the beige carpet ran right through the house, the two big beds in this room had colourful, throwover Indian blankets on them, and plain, white lamps beside them.

'See! No drapes!' Grant grinned at her. She had come up close to look into the room and for a moment she was only inches away from his face.

He took his hand away from the door and put it around her waist. Then, unhurriedly, he lowered his mouth to hers. The kiss was gentle and exploring.

Gemma wondered wildly what she would do if he became more insistent.

As his lips savoured hers, she felt herself responding, even putting her free hand up around his neck. When they separated, Grant's hand continued to hold her against him so that they were gazing deep into each other's eyes. Sighing, he dropped his hand, stood upright and stepped back.

'All right, Miss Prissy,' he said, 'you want me to let you go. OK, go and freshen up and I'll do the same. Meet you in the living-room in ten minutes.'

'Ten minutes!' Gemma was aghast. 'Make it twenty.'

'And I thought all that youthful beauty was natural,' he mocked as he turned into his own room.

Hurriedly, she lifted her bag on to the nearest bed, pulling out a black dress which showed her tan off to perfection. Going into the bathroom, she dropped her clothes on the floor, turned on the shower and drew the glass-panelled door after her. Her own reflection stared back at her from three sides. More of Sugar's taste, she thought, smiling, as she lifted her face to the warm, relaxing water.

She was ready in a quarter of an hour but Grant had beaten her to it and was sitting out on the deck with the door open and the ocean in front of him. Two tall glasses were beside him and he handed one to Gemma as she appeared.

'Hope you like margueritas,' he said. 'It's a little early, but as you can see, the sun is going down.'

'It's beautiful,' Gemma said, with feeling. The breakers seemed quieter now and the changing light cast the driftwood, and an unmoving heron down on the beach, into black silhouettes against the pink sky. They sipped in silence, appreciating the quiet beauty before them.

After a moment, Gemma said, 'Because I let you kiss me, please don't get the wrong idea. I'm holding you to your word — about this week-end.'

Grant's voice, when he replied, was deep and even, but it held a touch of anger. 'Nobody forced you, and I'm neither a rogue or a fool. You enjoyed that kiss as much as I did.'

Gemma got up and walked restlessly

to the deck rail. Below her, the sun's rays carried light from the horizon so that from where Grant sat, she appeared to be bathed in sunlight, but her expression was hidden from him. Not looking at him, she stared down into her drink as though it held secrets. Presently, having considered her words she said, 'I've no grounds for not trusting you — except that you are a Markham and, it seems, I own something you want. Do you deny that?'

Grant came towards her. It was strange, she thought irrationally, how menacing a big man could be when he silently loomed over one. He said, as though thinking about it carefully, 'Do I want something you have? Yes, I think you do.'

She was incensed. To admit that he wanted her physically was trivialising the whole question of her grandmother's inheritance. She said sharply, 'You know perfectly well that we're talking about my land. You want it — don't you?'

'I've told you. Yes.'

For some reason, a straightforward answer took the wind out of Gemma's sails. She said, a little lamely, 'I see.' Then, whipping up her previous resentment, she lifted her chin and asked sharply, 'And is that what all this is about?'

He looked furious. 'No, it's not. You must be well aware that you're a very attractive girl, whom I find interesting. That was true before I knew who you were.'

Gemma felt that she had found a loophole at last in what, on the face of it, looked eminently sensible. She said, with a touch of a sneer, 'But then, when you and your sister discovered who I was, I got dropped like a hot cake, didn't I?' He was silent and she pressed her advantage. 'Didn't I, Grant?'

'Yes.' He almost snarled at her and, at her slight recoil, came closer and reached for her hand. She held it away from him, knowing that too much proximity would bias the argument in his favour and she did not want to be swayed. She wanted the truth.

Grant turned away and went through the glass door into the house to pour himself another drink. When he returned, Gemma was standing with her back to him, gazing out across the ocean, feeling the warmth of the dying sun on her face and body. He came up behind her and encircled her waist with his arms, grasping the rail on either side of her.

'Let me go!' Gemma tried to wriggle out of his hold.

'No. This time we're going to get things straight — and you're going to listen.' He spoke into her hair as she defiantly continued to stand with her back to him.

'All right. If that's the way you want it, so be it. You don't have to look at me if you don't want to, but you're going to listen.

'I was very attracted to you when we met, you must have sensed that, and I'm not proud of the fact that we stayed away once we found out who you were. However, in mitigation, let me tell you something of the feelings between your grandmother and my family. The land she lived on was originally gained from my family by a trick.'

'What? I don't believe it. How can you stoop so low as to say a thing like that about an old woman who can no longer defend herself? I don't believe it.'

'Gemma, I've said you're going to listen to me.'

He had brought his hands to her waist and was holding her tightly. As she tried to break free, he held her firmly, speaking quickly and vehemently. 'Maybe it isn't any good telling you that it's the truth but my father didn't lie and he wasn't a man who bore a grudge. Anyone in the community would tell you that. Can't you see that the past doesn't really concern us now?

'For years, Ruth Lawrence hated our family and everyone in town knew of the feud. I'm telling you, Gemma, that I was pretty upset when I discovered you were her granddaughter. In a way we felt, Sugar and I, that we would be doing you a favour leaving you to her people.'

'What people? There was only the doctor, lawyer and Matt Fulton.'

'Then I'm sorry, but I didn't know that. It would, we thought, be expecting a lot of those close to her, to accept our help on your behalf.'

Gemma longed to point out that no-one had been close to Ruth but would not do so, because that smacked of disloyalty. She ached yet again for the lonely, old woman, even if, for the first time, a seed of doubt entered her head. Had Ruth been lonely and alone because she had chosen to be that way — or had she driven away anyone who had put out the hand of friendship to her?

She cried, 'Maybe that explains why you left me alone — but it doesn't explain why you came back into my life. Was it my irresistible attraction?'

Sarcastically putting the emphasis on 'irresistible', she was dumbfounded when he said quietly and seriously, 'Yes. It was.'

He raised his hands to her shoulders and Gemma twisted quickly and turned to face him. Unsteadily, she said, 'Do you expect me to believe that?'

Grant compressed his lips. He looked nothing like an admiring suitor, for he was frowning and he looked down into her face almost as though he disliked her. 'Why didn't you have the honesty to tell me your name that first night? It would have meant nothing to me at that point. Later I knew, or thought I knew, what you were after.'

'All right, so I made a hash of it,' he said resignedly. 'Shall we leave it now and get some dinner?' He let her go and moved away.

★ ★ ★

The sky had changed from pink to orange and the last remnants of sun and light were turning the driftwood into weird shapes. Grant, ever courteous, was holding the restaurant door open for her. Remembering the meal they had enjoyed at The Depot, she resolved to try and capture the mood they had had then.

The restaurant they went to was up the hill from the bay and situated so that each diner had a sea view. Both of them, Gemma thought, had decided to make an effort. She looked up at her smiling, handsome escort and thought that, if nothing else, he had added a new dimension to her life and, for that, at least, she must be grateful. If only she dared trust him!

When the wine was poured, Grant lifted his glass and held it up for a toast.

'To us,' he said.

Gemma, quick to match his mood, repeated, 'To us,' but when he put a hand across the table a little later to hold hers, she drew away.

Back at the house, before they went inside, he drew her once more to the front. 'Look at that,' he whispered, an arm around her shoulders and his head close to hers. 'It's an Oregon moon.' Together, they gazed at the black sky, the waves and the moonlight on the water.

'It's beautiful.' Gemma shivered as the light breeze lifted the loose folds of her white jacket.

Grant felt the movement and became solicitous.

'You're cold. Come on, we'll go in.' He opened the door and she walked ahead of him.

What now, she wondered, a tight little knot of apprehension in her stomach.

Grant began turning on low lamps. 'There's no need to pull the drapes here,' he said. 'Nobody but Father Neptune or an odd mermaid could see us.' He turned on a stereo and music filled the room.

Gemma looked around at the effect he was rapidly creating. Standing still in the middle of the room, she said baldly,

'You know, I can't help feeling that this is beginning to look rather sinister.'

'Sinister? I'd rather hoped I was making it look inviting.' He contrived to wear the hurt expression of a little boy.

'Oh, yes, you're certainly doing that,' Gemma agreed, 'but isn't this a rather clichéd, seduction scene?'

He grinned and then, coming to stand in front of her and leering horribly, asked, 'Wouldn't you like to change into something more . . . er . . . comfortable?'

'No, thanks, I'm perfectly comfortable,' she said, struggling not to laugh. Her thoughts were chaotic, though. Not only was he handsome, but he could make her laugh. One part of her chided the other. What was wrong with her, that she still mistrusted his intentions? Smiling, she let herself be directed to the couch. He stood over her, mock bowing and asking in a wildly over-British accent, if there was anything Modom desired? Upon her denial, he sat down beside her, as she had known he would, and his face sobered.

'I still want to kiss you, again.' His lips met hers.

Gemma felt her pulses race in time to the waves beating against the shore almost beneath them; the intensity of feeling left them both gasping and breathless. As he pulled back, to regain his composure, she leaped to her feet and almost ran to her bedroom door. He did not rise but gazed after her, with a look of longing, as she paused at the door.

Hoarsely, he said, 'I'm sorry. I should have known that would be a mistake.' He said pleadingly, 'Will you ever forgive me?'

Gemma could trust herself to say nothing, but mutely shook her head.

With her hand on the door knob, she added, 'I'm sorry, too.' Then, with his eyes following her, she went through the door and left him.

4

In the morning, Grant was the best of hosts. He had been to the store and had orange juice and coffee ready for her out on the veranda. His manner was easy and Gemma felt her shyness beginning to evaporate.

She told him she had slept well and appreciated the comfort of the luxurious bed.

'I'm glad to hear that,' he said. 'Now, where would Madam like to go for breakfast? There are plenty of places, including the one we went to for dinner, but if you're interested in the best hash browns, it's got to be Mike's Diner, just up the hill.'

'Sounds good to me.' Gemma felt rested and relaxed. Though she did not mean to tell him so, she had felt safe for the first time since the death of her grandmother. Secure in the belief that he would not intrude on her privacy, she had luxuriated in the joys of her own 'suite', enjoying the scented soap, the satin sheets and the plump pillows.

Once, she had half-woken, frightened by the sound of someone moving about in the next room. Then she had remembered. She was not alone in the woods and a sound in the next room meant only that she was protected from the unknown by a strong and capable man. Smiling to herself, she had turned over and gone straight back to sleep, until woken by the sunlight through the green curtains.

Now, though not particularly hungry, she was happy to go along with Grant's wish to treat her to an all-American breakfast. Once seated in the diner, with glasses of iced water before them, they bickered amicably about what she should try.

'I brought you here for the hash browns,' Grant insisted, 'and now you want waffles. How do you think you're going to keep that gorgeous figure if you eat all that syrup?'

His eyes swept over her as he spoke and she tilted her head, giving him a reproachful look.

He laughed. 'Sorry, I can't seem to get my mind off it. Do you know you look like a little blackbird with your head on the side like that?'

Gemma pointedly ignored this and continued to study the menu.

'What's a short stack?' she asked and Grant indicated a table where an enormously-fat man was tucking into a pile of thick pancakes, with a waterfall of syrup pouring down the sides. She decided that she didn't want that and mollified her escort by choosing one egg, sunny side up, and the famous hash browns.

As they ate, Grant mapped out the day's plans for her. 'We're going south. The highway really hugs the coastline, so it's a scenic route. We'll walk on a beach or two and, hopefully, collect some agates and jasper for you to keep.

'I'm going to drive up Cape Perpetua. It's two miles up and the view is spectacular. We'll get as far as Florence before we turn back. How does all that sound?'

'Wonderful.' Gemma smiled. She was a little worried, though. Why was he doing so much for her?

Grant saw her change of expression; he seemed to be able to tune into her moods so much that she fancied, uneasily, he could read her mind.

'Come back,' he said. 'You've gone away somewhere.' Then, as she didn't answer, 'Are you thinking about last night?'

She half-shook her head.

'Look, do I keep having to reassure you? I brought you here for a rest and a change. I'm going to do nothing that will spoil that.

'You're safe — as safe as you choose to be. If you choose differently — well, that's another story. But it's up to you.'

'I know — and I'm grateful.' Gemma remembered the secure feeling she had

had in the night. 'It's just — well, I wish I knew your intentions.'

'My intentions!' Grant looked astonished. 'That's a bit 'olde worlde', isn't it?'

'Oh, yes — no — I didn't mean that!' Horrified, she stammered, 'I just meant that I'm not sure if you are interested in me — or my land.'

Grant's face fell and he said, with more than a trace of coldness, 'If you're still doubting that, I can't imagine why you came away with me.'

She shivered, as though a warm blanket had been taken away and she was exposed. Somehow, she floundered on.

'I don't want to doubt; it would be much easier to take everything at face value but you've been, and are being, very kind, very thoughtful. I can't help wondering if it's me or — '

He was so furious that when he spoke, his voice held a suppressed anger she had never heard before.

'Look, Gemma, if you don't stop

worrying at your insecurities so much, there's really not much point in going on with this — this relationship. Can we drop it — or do we go home?'

She felt ashamed. After all he had done for her, how could she be so churlish? Shakily, she took a sip of water and said in a low voice, 'I'm sorry. It was my fault entirely for bringing it up.'

Instantly, Grant's smile was wide. 'Let's forget it,' he said lightly, and, in her relief, Gemma did not realise, until much later, that once again he had given her no assurances about his interest in her land.

The day was exactly as Grant had said. She exclaimed with admiration the miles of coast and the forests that could be seen on the way. Little cars snaked below them along the ribbon of road.

By afternoon, as they retraced their route, Gemma told Grant that she was beginning to feel quite punch-drunk with so many sights and such beauty.

'Every bend yields a new delight,' she said.

He turned his head. He said nothing but his smile showed how much he enjoyed her appreciation of his native state.

She chuckled. 'You really are a true Oregonian. I don't know how they managed to keep you in Europe so long.'

His smile was pensive. 'I wish they hadn't. I'd have seen more of my parents in their last few years.'

Gemma's quick sympathy was aroused and she put out her hand and touched his arm where it rested lightly on the steering wheel.

The road was straight at that point, with nothing coming in the opposite direction, and Grant's eyes, as he turned and looked at her, were hot. He said huskily, 'Are you looking for trouble, Miss Laurence?'

'No, I am not, Mr Markham,' she said hastily, glad she had been able to change his mood.

'Are you sure?' He was baiting her. 'Because it's a hot afternoon and if you want to fool around a little, it's my guess we could find a lonely place down on the beach real easy.'

Gemma adopted a broad, Southern accent and said severely, 'You-all tend to yuh drivin', Sir, an' don let sech thoughts fill yuh head.'

'Not bad,' Grant said consideringly. 'Not bad at all. But I think it had too much of the Scarlett O'Hara influence. Come to think of it, you even look like her.'

'Thank you,' Gemma said demurely, 'but I'll think about that tomorrow.'

Back at the house, it was with far less anxiety than the previous night that Gemma saw the fading of the sunlight. Again, Grant mixed drinks for them as they sat out to watch the sun disappear into the sea.

Somehow, after their first night alone together, she trusted him, but her head kept telling her things she did not want to hear.

'Just why is he being so nice?' 'Don't trust him!' 'What do you think your grandmother would say — or your mother for that matter?' 'What kind of girl are you, to be impressed because he's handsome, and rich?' She banished the thoughts and smilingly accepted another drink, determined to enjoy the moment.

'That dress you're wearing tonight matches your eyes exactly,' Grant had said the moment she had stepped out of the bedroom. She was wearing a filmy, blue creation, bought in London and never worn.

'Does it? I'm glad you like it.' Having bought it for that very reason, Gemma knew perfectly well that it matched her eyes. Holding the glass to her lips, she sipped and looked at him over the rim, innocently provocative. The sun had disappeared and been replaced by a young moon; the tide covered the sand bar, leaving a narrow strip of beach.

Grant reached for her glass, putting it down beside her on the deck. 'I think you've had enough,' he said, looking into her slightly-floating gaze. He looked repentant. 'I shouldn't have made them so strong.'

Gemma was offended. 'Are you saying I'm drunk? she asked, rather pugnaciously.

He was amused. 'Let's just say it would be a good idea to go for a walk. Come on.' He took her hand and drew her to her feet. 'We'll walk on the sand awhile.'

Gemma held back. 'We might get cut off by the tide,' she said, blinking at the now-black water and its foam-laced edges.

'We won't.' He was adamant. 'And if we do, I'll make you rescue me. Come on.' He pulled her towards the steps and led her firmly down.

The stars were beginning to emerge as they strolled across the length of the beach. 'Isn't it wonderful how much more sky there is here?' She had taken off her sandals and her bare feet relished the cold sand between her toes.

'More sky? Yes, I suppose there is.' Grant stared up at the expanse of diamond-studded darkness. 'You never see this if you live in a big city.'

'You never see this if you live amongst tall trees either,' Gemma countered.

A light breeze had begun to sweep in across the water and she shivered. He took off his jacket and placed it across her shoulders.

'Thank you.' Gemma smiled gratefully up at him, and his hands remained on her shoulders. Her smile faded. Plainly, he was going to kiss her, but he took his time, as though giving her a chance to refuse. As he lowered his head, the light was blotted out until he, and he alone, became her world. She was aware of nothing else. At some point, Grant's jacket fell from her shoulders.

By then he was kissing her face, her neck ... Even when she lost her balance and tumbled onto the sand, they were far too entangled to allow her to fall alone. Grant rolled over to draw her closer. But the tumble had sobered Gemma and broken the spell. Pushing him frantically away, she struggled to her feet crying, 'No, please.'

He looked dazedly up at her, but made no attempt to reach for her again. She stood, panting and dishevelled, stooping to pick up his jacket where it lay on the sand. Somehow, she felt guilty as she watched him, still sitting on the sand, put his head into his hands.

After a moment which seemed like hours, he seemed to pull himself together and stood, tall beside her. His smile deflected her fears. He was again her companion of the day, light and teasing, rather than the fiercely-passionate man of a minute before.

He took her hand and they began walking up the beach, retracing their steps. Gemma said softly, 'Are you angry with me?'

He continued to look straight ahead, but the grasp on her hand tightened.

'No. If anything, I'm angry with myself.'

Back at the house, Gemma turned to face him. Her voice a little wobbly, she said, 'Grant, I don't think I should have come with you this week-end. It's — it's too hard, for both of us.'

Grant sat on the arm of a couch. Drawing off one shoe, he tipped sand from it onto the carpet. He watched the sand falling and said nothing until it was all out. Then, still studying the little pile of sand and taking his time to answer, 'Would you like me to go?'

'No.' Gemma was quick to deny any such intention. 'And taking your shoe off like that was a silly thing to do. Someone has got to clear it up.'

'I didn't know you were the little housewife type,' he teased lightly. Then, raising his head he looked at her, and it was as though an electric current crossed the room between them. Trembling, she slipped his jacket off and laid it neatly along the back of the couch. She wondered why she felt like crying.

'Well, I guess we'd better go and eat.' He had absently tipped out the other shoe and there was an even bigger pile of sand on the carpet.

Without a word, Gemma fetched a dustpan and began to clear it up. Kneeling at his feet, she looked up at him after she had finished, unconsciously tipping her head questioningly on one side. He laughed and reached forward to ruffle her hair.

'You're doing your bird imitation again,' he said, before taking her hand once more and drawing her towards the door. 'I know a wonderful restaurant that serves the best clam chowder on the coast — and that's where we're going, right now.'

It certainly was wonderful soup, the best Gemma had ever tasted. They followed it with tacos, salad and carrot cake and by the time coffee came, she admitted to feeling full, as well as tired.

Grant looked at his watch as they left

the restaurant and told her that although the night was still young, he thought he'd better tuck her into bed before she dozed off. She gave him a prim look and said that, although she appreciated his offer, she really was quite capable of tucking herself up.

His offer was repeated later, outside her bedroom door. Holding her lightly by the shoulders, he looked down into her face, his own serious. With one finger, he traced its contours, as though memorising them. Then he tapped her gently on the tip of her nose.

'You're quite sure — about tucking you up?'

Gemma smiled, but her expression, too, was serious. She felt no fear, simply regret. 'Quite sure.' An impish twinkle came into her eyes. 'Don't take it personally — I don't doubt your expertise.'

He grinned and, letting her go, turned towards the bedroom door. 'If you should change your mind, just call out! Goodnight, Gemma.'

Later, as she lay, restless, in the big bed, she thought how easy it would be to get up and simply walk, lit by the moon, from her room to his.

She imagined herself melting into his arms — and there, she hurriedly brought her unruly imagination into line. Even then, she could not sleep, and after an hour of tossing and turning, other thoughts came. What good company he was, and yet, how cold he could be.

Before sleep finally overcame her, her last, conscious memory was his kindness during the day. That, surely, could not have been feigned?

'Grandmother,' she whispered softly into the darkness, 'I think you would have liked him.'

She seemed to hear Ruth angrily refuting such an outrageous suggestion. 'Me? Like a Markham? Never!'

5

On Sunday afternoon, when Grant drove Gemma home, they were both feeling healthy and relaxed from leisure, sun and the pleasure of each other's company. As he dropped her bags on the veranda of the cabin she said, 'Won't you come in for a while?'

'No.' Grant smiled into her eyes.

Unaccountably, she felt shy. Ridiculous, she chided herself. After the nights and days in the presence of this man, how could she be shy at the prospect of him being with her in her own home? She was sure he sensed how she felt, which added to her confusion.

He went on, 'I've a great deal of work to catch up on, back at my office. I'm going to go straight there and will probably be at my desk most of the night. If there is anything — ' He paused and looked round at the quiet peace of the cabin.

'If anything bothers you, please ring me.' He took his wallet out of his back pocket and produced a small, business card. As Gemma took it, he caught hold of her hand and drew it up so that he was holding it against his chest. For a moment he was still, looking down into her eyes. 'It's been good being with you.' His voice was deep and meaningful, his smile a little crooked, as he added, 'Maddening at times — frustrating at times — but good.'

Gemma returned the smile. 'For me, too. Thanks for everything.' It was hard to think he would go, leaving her alone in the forest. Why was it a prospect she dreaded? She'd known joy and sorrow in the cabin but at the moment a strange fear prevailed.

Grant was still looking down at her, her hand firmly nestled inside his. He seemed, once again, to know what she was thinking.

'Remember,' he urged, 'I'm not far away, only on the end of a phone.'

Bending his head, he opened the palm of the hand he held cupped in his and dropped a kiss on to it. Then, as though he would not be able to go at all if he did not go quickly, he turned and strode away.

With one look back he was gone, the car swirling away in a cloud of dust.

Gemma waved until the Cadillac was out of sight and then stood on the veranda, her bag at her feet. The noise of his going died slowly and was replaced by stillness and woodland sounds.

A jay cackled, and a small animal chittered amongst the trees nearby. She watched a chipmunk scurry across a branch before she picked up her bag and went inside.

Grant's business card was still in her hand. It was printed in gold on a cream background and had a tiny engraving of a fir tree at the side. It had his home and business addresses, both with telephone numbers. She smoothed her fingers across it and placed it carefully on the pine chest in the living room. Somehow, having it there made her feel more secure.

The sound of footsteps, tramping across the wooden boards, startled her. She flew to the door and breathed a sigh of relief at the sight of the big, burly form of Matt Fulton.

Momentarily, he looked surprised to see her, but recovered his usual stolid expression, saying heavily, 'Hi, Gemma. Just came to see if there's anything . . . '

It was heartening to have a visitor so soon after coming home. Gemma said brightly, 'No, not as far as I know, but I'm pleased to see you. Do sit down, Matt, and I'll get a couple of beers from the fridge.'

He nodded and sat on a wicker chair that groaned heavily under his weight. She saw him look at her grandmother's rocker. In an attempt to lay any ghosts, she sat in it when she came back with the drinks and cookies.

Matt took a swig of the beer and wiped his mouth on the sleeve of his checked shirt. 'You been away?' he asked.

'Yes. I went to the coast for the week-end.' Gemma wondered uneasily if he knew with whom, but there were no more questions for a while. They both sat and contemplated the peaceful beauty around them.

'Your car,' Matt said eventually. 'It needs a few things doing to it. Shouldn't drive it without.'

'It does?' Gemma was startled. 'How do you know? Is it making the wrong noises or something?' she asked, concern in her voice.

Matt drank deeply before replying. He seemed to be consider his words, but he was always a slow speaker. Finally, he came out with, 'Nope. Knew Ruth didn't bother much with servicing. Mostly, I gave it a bit of an overhaul now and then. So, when I came up yesterday, I took the time to have a look. Got most of the parts at my place. I'll come tomorrow and fix it up for you.'

'Oh, thanks, Matt. I simply hadn't thought about it. I've just driven the poor old thing without checking anything except the petrol — I mean gas — and oil and tyres. They're so good here, about things like cleaning the windscreen whenever you go into a service station. I should have remembered it would need more attention sometimes. Are you sure you don't mind doing it?'

'Course not. Be a pleasure.'

Gemma looked uncertainly at him for a moment. She knew her grandmother had paid him for his work, but found it difficult to broach the matter of money. She said, falteringly, 'Whatever the cost of the parts and labour is, I'll leave it to you.'

His laconic, 'Don't need to worry about the bucks but if it'll make you feel better, I'll tell you when I finish and we can settle up,' seemed to put an end to the matter.

Gemma, somewhat embarrassed, said nervously, 'Yachats is a lovely bay. The whole coast is really beautiful.'

'Yes,' Matt agreed. 'Good for a day trip. Don't take more'n an hour or so to get there.'

He was looking at her, as though expecting an explanation of why she had stayed away so long.

Gemma felt, a little resentfully, that she had no obligation to explain to him why she had been away but she still heard herself saying, 'A — a friend invited me, and I think it was good for me to get away from the cabin for a while.'

'I guess so.' Matt nodded his head. He placed the empty beer can down on the table. 'D'you mind tellin' me who you was with?'

Gemma was immediately angry. 'Yes, I do mind. What right have you to ask me such a question?'

Matt looked taken aback. He straightened up and put out a placatory hand against her obvious indignation, and, for once, hastened into speech.

'Got no right at all, don't you think I know that? But there ain't nobody else hereabouts to keep an eye on you, and I'm certain your grandma woulda asked you a question like that if she'd still bin around.'

Gemma's anger died as quickly as it had arisen. The man meant well and it was true that she had no-one to advise her. To him, she must appear like a child.

'I'm sorry, Matt,' she said more calmly. 'I know you have my interests at heart. However, I am perfectly capable of managing my own affairs. Who I was with is no-one's business but mine.'

He said nothing for a second or two but she sensed he was unwilling to leave the matter there. He blurted out abruptly, 'That car of yours, maybe that weren't my affair neither, and I coulda let you just drive it into town one day an' get yourself in trouble.'

'That isn't fair,' she cried. 'It's an entirely different thing and to bring it up at the same time is — ' She sought for words to express her feelings and finished sharply, 'Emotional blackmail.'

Matt looked flummoxed. 'Don't know what you mean by that, but there's talk in town that you were with that Markham guy. He's after you, and I guess everybody knows why. If them Markhams can't get what they want easy, they mean to get it anyways. That's how they are. Only, I'm not goin' to stand by and see you taken for a ride.'

Gemma was speechless. How did anybody know about her relationship with Grant? Was this what small-town living was like, the total loss of one's private life? In a few, terse sentences she told Matt exactly what she thought of the intrusion.

She stood up and angrily gave him a brief account of her weekend, ending with, 'I'll make friends with whom I wish and I won't judge anyone on the grounds of an old feud.'

Matt's face had reassumed its usual

stoic expression. He got to his feet, saying woodenly, 'OK, but don't say nobody warned you. They're a bad lot, and if Ruth was still alive he wouldn't be allowed to set one foot on her property. Not one foot.'

Gemma could only sit and glare after him as he stomped off. After he reached the path in the woods which led to his house, he turned and called, as though there had been no disagreement between them, 'Be round tomorrow, Gemma, to fix the car, and anything else you find for me to do.' With a wave of his hand, he had disappeared through the trees and undergrowth, leaving her to stand and drum her fingers on the rail.

The day was spoiled of course. All her doubts resurfaced. During the last two days, she had pushed them to the back of her mind and had simply enjoyed being in Grant's company. Now she found herself, once more, mulling over his motives. He had been so attentive, so loving, never forcing himself on her. Was that the behaviour of a 'bad lot'?

By the time Gemma had tortured herself with thoughts like this for a few hours, she was heartily wishing for some other company than her own. When the phone rang later in the evening, she picked it up expecting that it would be an international call from her mother. When, instead, Grant's deep voice said, 'Gemma, are you all right?' her heart lurched so much that she was plunged into nervousness, and began to talk too fast. When she dried up at last, he said sharply, 'You're not all right. What is it?'

She remembered how hopeless it was, trying to hide her mood from him. 'Why do you always know everything about the way I'm feeling?'

He laughed. 'Call it intuition.'

'Well, I think it's a very sinister quality.'

'Thanks.' Grant did not appear to be flattered. 'But I'm only aware of your moods — no-one else's.'

There it was again, she thought confusedly, that closeness that he managed to create between them. But, if he understood her, then it was not reciprocal, for try as she might, she could not fathom him at all. He continued, 'You haven't told me yet, what it is that's worrying you. Are you going to?'

Gemma was tempted to refuse but capitulated, because she really did want to bring it out into the open.

'Matt Fulton's been here. He told me that it's common knowledge in town, that you and I are — well — about us seeing each other.'

'I see.' Grant's tone became cold and she wondered whether she should have stayed silent. 'That isn't all of it, is it?' he asked.

'No,' she agreed unhappily. 'But I can't repeat . . . ' She tailed off.

'Don't worry, I can guess the rest.'

She realised, desolately, that when he was cold like this, she felt abandoned. Wretchedly, she said, 'I'm sorry. I don't know what to think.'

'Don't you? Then it seems that you can't bring yourself to trust me.' He was remote — suddenly a complete stranger.

'I do trust you, in some ways, you know I do, especially after the weekend. How could I do otherwise? But when he told me . . . '

Grant's tone was icy. 'Gemma, there is nothing I can do or say, so it seems, to prove that I'm interested in you, not your bit of land.'

Illogically, she felt called upon to defend her inheritance. She said, 'It's more than a bit of land.'

He laughed mirthlessly. 'Yes, I know exactly how much more. I know the acreage, I know the trees, and I know how useful it would be to me and my firm. Is that what you wanted to hear?'

Gemma gasped, 'No,' in a small voice.

There was silence on the end of the line. When he spoke again, each word was clipped and precise. 'If you believe that our relationship is based purely on that, I'm sorry for your lack of perception. All I can say is that one day I hope you wake up to the fact that I am not a villain!'

Gemma said nothing. Her throat was full, and unshed tears were stiffening her face muscles. The stranger on the other end of the line said, 'Goodnight' in the same distant voice.

She heard him wait for a reply, and managed to whisper, 'Goodnight' before the click of the receiver told her he was gone.

Listlessly, she went to bed. Never before had she felt so alone. She did not know, luckily for her peace of mind, that she was not alone at all. The unseen watcher had returned.

6

'See that?' Matt pointed to a tree stump fifty yards from where he was working on the car next morning. Gemma had brought him a drink and was perched on the grass, keeping him company while he took a break. The sun had been up some time and, although it was cool in amongst the trees, the clearing was already over-warm for comfort. Matt wiped his greasy face with a hand, holding an oily rag as he pointed.

'It's just a stump, isn't it?'

'Take a closer look.' Matt dropped down beside her on the grass and lifted a mug from the tray.

Obediently, Gemma uncurled her long legs and walked across to the stump. As she peered down at it she called excitedly, 'Oh, I see what you mean. There's a tiny, little Christmas tree growing right out of the stump.'

She bent and stroked the small, green branches, whispering softly, 'Don't worry, little tree, I won't cut you down when Christmas comes. You must have struggled really hard to get rooted there.'

As she walked back to where Matt sat, his back against the thick, notched bark of a fir, she said, 'Isn't it a wonderful sight? Thanks for pointing it out to me.'

He put down his empty mug and got back onto his feet, wiping his hands on the back of his old blue jeans.

'My pleasure. Guess it's going to take more time than I thought to fix that car. Could be maybe a day or two.'

'Oh, really?' Gemma's face fell. 'That means taking up a lot of your time. Are you sure you don't mind?' When he shook his head, she added, 'It also means I'm stranded here.'

'Mebbe your friend'll come and take you out.' Matt's face was buried under the lifted bonnet of the car but his tone was unmistakably sarcastic.

121

Gemma flushed, and bit back an angry retort. What was the point of trying to convince Matt, when she herself was still a prey to so many doubts? What could she say that would change his mind about Grant, anyway? 'Markham' was clearly a dirty word in his vocabulary so she ignored the tone of his voice and answered lightly, 'I expect he will, if I ask him. And I expect you would, too, if I asked you.'

Matt emerged from the depths of the car. He looked suspiciously at her as he slowly rubbed grease on to a piece of piping he had lifted from the engine. He said, 'You know I would. Anywhere you want to go.'

'Good. I might take you up on that tomorrow. By the way, Matt, how did you know the car needed attention?' Her voice was entirely without guile or accusation but the piece of pipe dropped from his hand. He leaned down to pick it up and his deeply-sunburned face was even redder when he stood up again.

His voice, when he spoke, was apologetic. 'Guess I should have told you that I had a key. Ruth trusted me to take care of anything that needed doing. I kinda got into the habit of checking it out. Knew you were away, so I took a look under the hood.'

Gemma felt mildly suprised. 'You knew I was away?' she queried.

'Yes, I came calling. Nobody home and the car just sitting there. So I figured you had to be away.'

'Oh, I see.' Gemma chuckled. 'You're a real detective, Matt.' She wished that he wouldn't stare at her with such intensity, wondering again how it was that her grandmother had so enjoyed the company of this man.

There was a matter she felt she had to broach. Haltingly, she began, 'Matt, it's been bothering me that my grandmother was so indebted to you and yet didn't — didn't remember you at all, in her will. If there's any way I can make it up to you . . . I wish

. . . Oh, dear, I'm afraid I'm not saying this very well.'

Matt said, cutting across her stumbling sentences, 'Don't think I can do much more to this, today.' With finality, he shut down the bonnet and turned towards her, still ignoring what she had said. 'Mind if I go inside and wash up?'

Without waiting for an answer, he went into the cabin and she followed, wondering if she had embarrassed him, but wishing he would at least acknowledge her attempt to bring the subject into the open.

When he returned from the bathroom looking considerably cleaner, he seemed reluctant to leave and she saw, with a sinking heart, that he was lingering. That being so, she decided to reopen the matter of the will.

'I'm sorry if you don't want to talk about it,' she said, with a little lift of her chin, 'but whether we like it or not, we should discuss it.'

'Nothing to say,' he grumbled, ill at ease, but making no effort to escape.

'Isn't there? I don't think you're speaking the truth, Matt. Until I came on the scene, you were her only friend. You surely must have had expectations.'

He shifted uncomfortably in his chair. 'OK, if you're goin' to dig at me, when I'd rather let it rest, then I guess I'll say the thing clear. She told me, more'n two years ago, that she had a granddaughter back in England. Trouble was, she'd never met you, and she knew me. Knew I loved this place.' His eyes swept around the cabin and through the open doors to the clearing around it.

Gemma said slowly, 'You, too. Everyone seems to love it. But loving the land and the trees causes bad feeling between people.'

As though the words were dragged out of him, Matt answered, 'Isn't loving it that makes bad feelin'. It's wantin' to own it.'

Gemma leaned towards him, struck by the truth of what he was saying.

'Yes, you're right. That's exactly what

it is.' Then, alarmed by the look in his eyes, she drew back. 'But I didn't ever have any thoughts of owning it.'

'You own it, anyway, whether you thought about it or not.' His tone was almost scornful, as though he could not believe in such innocence. 'You must've known you had a gran over here who owned a lot of land.'

'I didn't. Even after she died, I didn't know she had much of value.'

'Well, anyhow, you kin see why I didn't believe it was ever going to be mine. Only thing was . . . ' he paused and looked away, ' . . . she used to say that she'd leave the cabin and the piece around it to you.'

'And the rest?' Gemma prompted.

He studied his fingernails. 'To me,' he said flatly, and instantly raised his head to stare into her eyes. 'That way the Markhams would never get it.'

Gemma let out an appalled breath and sat back. No wonder, she thought, that he had sometimes seemed strange and disgruntled. He couldn't help but

126

be a man with a grievance. She had come along and, within six weeks, without even trying, she had taken away what he had counted as his.

'Oh, Matt, I'm sorry. And I suppose it was a sort of promise.' She swallowed. 'My grandmother probably thought she could ask anything of you because in the end, it would be yours.'

'Ruth and me, we understood each other fine.' He had risen to his feet and walked restlessly to the window as though he did not want to sit close to Gemma any more. 'Until you came along.' The final words seemed forced out of him.

'I know.' Gemma felt wretched. 'You must hate me.'

Matt continued to stand, looking out the window. Gemma had come up behind him, anxious to express her regret, but at these words he turned towards her and his voice, when he spoke, was thick.

'No, I don't hate you,' he said and

she recognised the look in his eyes. It was raw desire.

Horrified, Gemma stepped back but not quickly enough. Matt could move fast for such an apparently clumsy man. He had hold of her with one arm and with the other held both her hands behind her. She was defenceless and, try as she could, she could not struggle free.

'Let me go. What do you think you're doing?' Fear lent a shrillness to her voice.

'Gemma, you and me, we could put everything right. Together, it wouldn't matter who had what. It'd be ours.' His face was so close that his breath was hot upon her cheek.

Trapped, she turned her head from side to side, knowing he meant to kiss her, dreading it.

'You're hurting me. Let me go,' she cried out, but his only answer was to push her back against the wall and pinion her arms at her sides. When he bent his big head and greedily took her lips, she closed her eyes and tried desperately to remain totally immobile.

When Matt finally lifted his face away from hers and gazed down at her, she was totally still and looking back at him with a self-control that baffled him. She managed to say in a cool, detached little voice, 'What do you suppose my grandmother would think were she to see you treating me like this?'

Matt drew back a little and looked round the room, as though Ruth's ghost might be behind him. At least he seemed ready to listen. Instinct told her she must not plead, that pleading would merely inflame the mixture of desire and angry resentment that he felt. It was, therefore, with a show of arrogance that she said icily, 'Is this an example of American manners?'

Releasing one hand, Matt took her chin in an unmercifully-hard grasp and growled, 'Just what do you mean by that? You go away with Markham and stay with him, but I'm not good enough for you. Till I knew that, I thought . . . '

'You thought what? What I do with my life is no business of yours, nor anyone else's. I have a right to choose my friends. I'm grateful to you for many things, Matt, but right now, you've overstepped the mark. We'll talk sometime soon, but at the present moment, I want you to leave.'

For what seemed long moments, he stood gazing at her, his chin down and a look of belligerence on his face. He said slowly, 'You think you've got the upper hand? Has it occurred to you that we're all alone out here?'

'Of course it has occurred to me,' Gemma was thankful that no tremor crept into her voice, 'but I don't believe that you've lost all sense of decency and honour. The Matt who was a friend of my grandmother would not, I think, have hurt either her or me. Am I right?' She waited, standing straight and looking directly at him, not knowing whether her arrow would hit the target or go wide.

Eventually, Matt's eyes dropped under her gaze. Turning away, he grumbled, 'You're enough to madden a man, for sure.' He moved to the door. He said, as though the words were dragged out of him, 'If I come back tomorrow, to finish fixing the car, do I get thrown out?'

'No, of course not.' Now that the danger was, apparently, past, Gemma was slightly ashamed. Knowing his disappointment, she almost pitied him. 'Some time we must talk. But for now, please leave.'

'OK.' He stepped out on to the wooden deck and she heard his footsteps descending the stairway.

Not until she was sure he was well away from the clearing was she able to give way to her emotions. Then, with a sob of mingled fury and self-pity, she flung herself on to the couch and began pounding the cushions.

'I hate them all,' she cried out loud. 'They all want this place — and me

— for the worst possible reasons.

'I hate them all, and I wish I'd never come here or inherited anything. It's brought me nothing but fear and sorrow!'

7

After a moment, reaction set in, and Gemma curled up on the couch, hugging the cushions and rocking. What was she going to do now? It was well-nigh impossible to stop Matt coming over to the cabin. It had been his second home for years and been snatched from him.

Grant had told her to ring him if she had any troubles. Her hand reached out for the telephone, before she stopped and drew it back again. Yes, she could talk over her fears with him and she was sure it would help to share her worries, but what could he possibly do? The last thing she wanted was a confrontation between the two men.

In any case, Matt had not exactly done anything. It would be difficult to describe the menace she sensed was there, without sounding like a naive schoolgirl.

Anyway, how unfair it would be to forget the friendship between Matt and her grandmother. No, the only answer was to make it clear that any repeat of today's episode would mean the end of his freedom to visit.

She got up and went to the kitchen to make herself a drink. As she took the steaming mug on to the deck the telephone rang.

'Hello, Gemma speaking.'

'This is Dan Wrotham. We met at my office in town.'

'Yes, I remember. You're the lawyer dealing with my grandmother's estate.' She recalled him clearly, a precise grey-haired man who had emigrated to the States from Tunbridge Wells some twenty years ago. She asked eagerly, 'Do you have some news for me?'

'I do indeed. There has been a surprising development. Our office doesn't deal with real estate, and I must admit I was not entirely receptive to the idea that I should be the one to communicate this to you.'

Gemma waited, wondering if he would ever get to the point. He seemed to be expecting some comment from her. 'Please go on,' she said impatiently.

'Yes, well, there has been an offer for the wooded acreage which you now own, with the house on which you live; an offer which, I believe, is extremely generous. Nevertheless, I must impress upon you that you need advice, and the recommendation I would make is to contact Trusthouse Realty, who deal in land as well as housing.'

He gave her the address of the firm before adding, rather pompously, 'The sum is a very large one. If you accept, you will be a rich woman.'

He named the figure and Gemma gasped, stunned. Her voice shook as she asked, 'Isn't that an extraordinarily large figure for such an amount of land?'

Dan Wrotham wrapped up his answer in a hundred different whys and wherefores. Eventually, however, with the proviso that the real estate people would give her a more accurate assessment, he did concede that it was an amazingly high offer.

With a sinking heart, she asked, guessing what the answer would be, who had made the offer. Dan Wrotham confirmed that it was, as he described him, the local timber baron, Grant Markham.

'Thank you, Mr Wrotham. I'll find out more and be in touch with you again.'

Quickly, she put down the phone, not trusting herself to carry on a rational conversation any longer, and for long moments afterwards, she sat staring into space. How could Grant be so crass? Was she some sort of deserving case, that he should try to buy her inheritance as such an inflated price?

She got up and went out onto the deck, staring at the trees around and above. Her trees, she thought proprietorially. What he was offering her was like winning a sweepstake, or lottery. With that kind of money, she could invest it, live wherever she liked, buy clothes, a new car; have all the things she had never been in a position to have. It was everybody's dream. But how dare he not talk to her in person? How dare he make such an offer to her lawyer?

If she accepted, there would be no more worries about being alone in the woods, or her future. The money would make it possible to help the family in England, too. Did she really have any right to refuse, knowing this? On her own account it might be easy to resist temptation, but was it fair on them? Sighing, she plumped down into the rocking chair and immediately remembered, with horrid clarity, her grandmother's last plea not to sell to the Markhams. Sudden tears rose to her eyes, but she blinked them back. She must think, not cry.

The sun chose that moment to break through the branches above, and bathe her in golden rays. Gemma felt the warmth on her back and stood up, lifting her face to it. In that instant, she made a momentous decision — no-one was going to wrest her heritage from her. Grant should be taught a lesson.

She went back indoors and dialled Grant's office number. As she listened to the ringing, a new and unwelcome thought came into her mind. If she had accepted, he would have expected her to return to England. Was that how he wanted it — that she leave Oregon for ever?

There was no time to speculate further as a female voice identified itself as Claudia, Mr Markham's secretary. Gemma asked to speak to Mr Markham, but was told he was 'in conference'. Upon giving her name and a request for him to call back, the secretary promptly replied, 'There's no need — Mr Markham is available now. I'll put him right on.'

Plainly, Grant had left instructions that she was to speak to him whenever she called. Gemma didn't know whether to feel honoured or be amused. When he came on she said decisively, while cursing the way just hearing him could make her heartbeat quicken, 'I'd like to talk to you, but if it's inconvenient I'm quite happy to have you call me back.'

He laughed, sounding relaxed and good-humoured. 'It's not at all inconvenient. The 'conference' excuse is just a ploy my secretary uses to everyone, unless they're on my list of special people I want to get hold of.'

'I see. I'm flattered.' Somehow, she was finding it hard to broach the reason for her call.

Her courage seemed to have ebbed. He, apparently, had forgotten that she must have called him for a reason, and went on, eagerly, 'Perhaps that's not quite what I meant to say, although it's true. I'd love to get hold of you!'

The tone of the conversation was wrong. Gemma wondered how she was going to force it back onto a business-like footing. Without waiting for her to speak, he said, 'Tomorrow, I'm having Sugar, and Jim and the boys, out to my place for the day. Sugar wants to meet you again — she feels bad about what happened. I told her I'd get you there if I had to drag you. So I'm coming by your place about eleven o'clock. The swimming pool is heating up nicely. Will you come? I'd love to show you my home.'

Gemma thought longingly of a leisurely day by the swimming pool, in the company of Grant and Sugar. True, she had been angry at Sugar, but she could understand the other girl's loyalties, and it sounded as though she wished to make amends. But to accept this invitation at the very moment she was about to turn down his offer was impossible.

She hardened her heart and her voice. 'No, Grant, I'm sorry, I can't.' Before he could interrupt, she went on hurriedly, 'I rang for a specific purpose. My lawyer, Dan Wrotham called.'

'Oh.' His voice, too, had changed.

'I'd hoped we could keep any financial dealings separate from our . . . ' There was a pause as he searched for the right word. 'Social ones,' he finished.

'I'm sorry, I don't agree with that.' Gemma was much more in command of herself now. 'We can't keep such things apart, and I don't see any point in negotiating through a third party. He told me you had made an offer for my land. It's a very generous offer. Thank you very much, but I've decided to refuse.'

'What?' His voice was loud and he sounded shocked.

'I've told you. I'm turning it down.'

'You must be mad!' He sounded amazed.

'It's my choice. I hadn't even put it up for sale, so why should you suppose I wanted to sell anyway?'

'Gemma, if you think anyone else will offer that much — or if you think I'll go higher, I tell you now, you're in cloud cuckoo land.'

'Oh!' Gemma gasped, furious at his

arrogant assumption that she was holding out for a higher price. 'Don't you understand plain English? I'm not interested. I said I wasn't selling — not now, not ever! I live here and I'm going to stay, whatever you think about it.'

'On what?' Grant demanded. His voice was infinitely scathing, as he shot the question at her.

'What do you mean, on what?' She hated herself for sounding so defensive.

'What are you going to live on? There's no income to be derived from that land. You may or may not know it, but Ruth Lawrence sold off bits around the edge as building plots, just to avoid selling to us. Because of that, I have five houses in the middle of my timber area.'

'Well, if that isn't just too bad.' Gemma's voice was even more sarcastic than his; she was angrier than ever, after the reference to her grandmother.

Hardly aware of what she was saying, she snapped, 'Thanks for giving me that idea. If that's the only way to live on it, that's what I'll do. You can expect to see more houses springing up in the middle of your trees, as soon as I can arrange it. So tough luck, Mr Landowner Markham, and goodbye.'

She slammed the receiver down hard and found she was breathing fast. Her fury was, she felt, justified. Presently, though, she calmed down and began to regret her last outburst. It hadn't been fair to make threats, but he'd been so arrogant, as though ordinary people wanting homes didn't count.

Going into the kitchen area, she realised she was hungry and tried to forget her frustration in cooking her supper. As there were only eggs and a tired piece of cheese in the fridge, she had to settle for an omelette. Reaching up to a high shelf for her grandmother's old copper omelette pan, she dropped two of the eggs.

'Oh, blast, nothing's going right today!' she said aloud. If only, Gemma thought miserably, the car was not out of action, she could at least have jumped into it and taken off for town.

She switched on the TV for company. What must it have been like, in pioneer days, she mused, before the advent of electrical gadgets — nothing but lamplight and shadows, cold and hard work? Although Ruth had pretended to despise the television, there were a few programmes she enjoyed watching.

Now, nearly every channel Gemma tried was in the middle of a noisy advertisement. Sighing, she finally found a soap opera, but it was hard to get interested in the activities of such a strange bunch of people. Still, she left it on when she returned to the kitchen, admitting to herself that voices other than her own were a big help in keeping worries at bay.

She put the omelette on a tray, and poured herself a glass of wine. The serial on the screen had changed to a game show. A big wheel, with large sums of money on it in neon lights, was being rotated by a fat man who had already won thousands of dollars. It reminded Gemma, of the offer Grant had made her.

With dusk falling outside, the cabin felt very isolated and she wondered whether she had been too hasty. What, indeed, was she going to live on? Had it been pique which had made her refuse? There was very little money in the bank and she couldn't take a job in the States — not without many problems and a lot of red tape.

Her glass in her hand, she sat and gazed, unseeingly, at the noisy, colourful programme, marshalling thoughts of a future which was based here in this beautiful but lonely house.

She must decide, whether the threat of Matt Fulton was a real, or imagined one — in any case, she had to be freed from it. To be mobile was a necessity. It was stupid to wait for Matt to fix the car, as though he was the only one able to. Feeling much better for making this decision, she looked through the telephone book and rang a garage at the north end of town.

The man agreed to come out and take a look next day, but warned her he might have to tow it back to his workshop.

'Fine,' Gemma agreed, 'as long as I can get it on the road.'

That done, she sat and drafted an advertisement which she intended to insert in the local paper, for a female lodger. If she were successful, not only would that give her some company, but it would mean another car on the premises, and bring in some income. She wondered why she hadn't thought of it before, and realised that until she had made the decision to stay, she had not felt in control of her life. Now, she did. At least she had that to thank Grant for.

As darkness deepened round the cabin, Gemma wrote a long letter home. She told them about the weekend at the beach, and the beauties of the Oregon coast, but left out any mention of the offer for the land. She went up the gallery steps before midnight. Tomorrow, when the garage man came, she'd beg a lift into town, and see the people at the Immigration and Social Security offices; maybe find out about the possibilities of getting a job. Her mind busied itself with plans for decorating and refurnishing the house. Maybe she'd get a puppy or a kitten. As she fell asleep, she began, finally, to feel secure in her little world.

The moon had been riding the heavens for hours when the key in the downstairs door was softly turned. It gave no more than a small click. The feet that trod, shoeless, up the gallery steps were sure and purposeful. Gemma had been asleep for a long time when her bedroom door was softly opened. The intruder stood by the bed and looked at her.

Moonlight crept across the room, to reveal her mass of hair and creamy bare shoulders. Presently, having looked his fill, but making no move to touch her, the man went noiselessly back the way he had come.

Gemma stirred and muttered, but did not wake. She was dreaming about Ruth, and in her dream the old lady was valiantly holding back a mad dog who was trying to attack her granddaughter.

8

'Gemma, where are you?' The footsteps on the deck, and Grant's unmistakable voice, took her by surprise next morning. What was he doing here? After the way they had spoken on the phone, Gemma could not believe that he had simply turned up. Still sleep-befuddled, she pulled on a cotton housecoat and went out onto the gallery, tugging at the ribbons that drew it together.

Tall and handsome, his blond hair sunbleached to an even lighter gold, Grant stood on the deck, outside the patio doors, looking impatiently through the glass. He wore an oversized, beige, linen jacket over a black T-shirt and slacks. Hearing the movement on the gallery, he looked up and a broad smile came over his face.

'I'm coming,' she called, and went

149

quickly down to open the doors. He stepped in, still grinning at her slightly owlish blinking, and obvious confusion. She drew the housecoat self-consciously around her.

He said teasingly, 'It's nine thirty, my sleeping beauty, and I've come to take you out to my place.'

'What?' Gemma gasped up at him, trying to fan the remains of yesterday's wrath. It was hard going when he was standing so close.

'I didn't think — oh, for goodness' sake, Grant, you must have known I didn't expect you to turn up after the phone call yesterday. You're mad!'

'Am I?' His voice was low, his eyes caressing. He made no move to touch her but it was as though she was being held and embraced. 'If I am, you're the reason.

'Now — ' His voice became brisk. 'Stop standing there, looking so tantalising.' Just for a moment, his gaze dropped from her face and lingered on the curves visible at the top of the wrap she held around her.

'I'll wait here.' He spread himself lengthways on the couch and picked up a magazine. 'Do whatever it is you do to make yourself presentable to the outside world. As far as I'm concerned, you look perfect.'

Gemma put a hand to her disarrayed hair. The housecoat loosened and she quickly brought her hand down again and grasped the edges. Feeling foolish, she said sharply, 'Grant, this is ridiculous. I told you yesterday — I made it clear I wasn't coming.'

'So you did,' he agreed affably, 'but I decided, that if you got difficult, I'd drag you. Is that how you want it?'

Gemma eyed him apprehensively. 'You wouldn't,' she said uncertainly, wondering if he were really capable of carrying out his threat.

'Try me.' Grant opened his eyes wide, and parted his lips expectantly as though he relished the challenge.

She bit her lip, and for a tense moment there was silence as they measured each other's strength, like combatants circling warily in an arena. Gemma's resolution was weaker because, in fact, she wanted very much to go with him, rather than spend another dismal day in the cabin. She was also honest enough to admit to herself that she had great curiosity about his home. But how could she give way with honour?

Grant settled the problem for her. Blithely, he slid off the couch, looked at his watch, and said decisively, 'I'm giving you a count of ten. After that, I'm picking you up and throwing you across the saddle of my horse — metaphorically speaking. Ready or no, here we go. Ten,' he counted loudly, 'nine, eight, seven and a half . . . ' His look at her, between each number, was brim full of mischief.

In spite of herself, Gemma began to giggle. 'All right, all right, you win. But you'll have to wait while I shower and dress.'

'Consider it done.' He threw himself

back on to the couch, grumbling. 'You were too easy. Throwing you over my saddle would suit my notions of male superiority. I was hoping you'd put up more of a fight.'

'Were you, indeed?' Gemma was at the top of the gallery now and feeling a little braver for the distance. She was fairly sure he would not invade the privacy of her bedroom, and looked down at him. 'Actually, I think I've changed my mind.'

He moved like lightning and stood, with one foot on the bottom step. Suddenly, unexpectedly, he spread his arms and misquoted wildly, 'Juliet, Juliet, wherefore art thou, Juliet?'

Gemma dissolved into mirth. 'I thought you'd had an English education,' she scoffed.

'I wasn't bluffing — I'll come and get you,' he shouted back in his usual voice.

'Don't bother,' she answered hastily, for he had taken two more steps upwards. 'If you're going to use Shakespeare, I can refuse you nothing.

Although,' she added, just before she disappeared from his view, 'I do think you're a little old to be Romeo!' She could hear him chuckling, as she went into the bedroom and began dragging clothes out of the closet.

She pulled on a pair of white trousers and a striped yellow and white top. Snatching up her bathing suit and a big beach towel, she went out on to the gallery.

A thought struck her. She had asked the garage to see to the car and now she would not be able to meet them.

'Grant, I've just remembered something.' She was having trouble with a pair of earrings, as she came down the stairs to him.

Seeing her struggles, he came towards her. 'Here, let me.' He took the gaily-coloured, hanging parrots, holding them up. 'These are fun,' he commented, aiming the little gold hook whilst grasping her ear-lobe with the other hand. Trying to hide the fact that his touch ignited something within her,

Gemma stood still as he fixed them.

Then, his hands dropped to her shoulders, as he looked seriously down at her. 'Do you know what I'd like to see in those ears?' He didn't wait for her reply. 'Emeralds — they'd suit your colouring beautifully.'

She laughed. 'Emeralds are a bit beyond my pocket. Perhaps you'd also like me to wear a diamond tiara?'

'I would,' he agreed, refusing to change back to his former, bantering tone. 'Believe me, if you say the word, you'd have whatever jewels you fancy.'

As Gemma looked up at him, the sparkle left her expression. Was he being tactless enough to refer to his extravagant offer for her estate? If not, what did he mean? She dared not speculate. Ignoring the remark completely, she told him about the garage-man calling for her car.

'No problem,' he said instantly. 'We'll drop by there. Leave them your ignition key and my telephone number. Then, if something major is wrong with the old heap, they can call you before fixing it.'

She would have liked to have taken issue with his scathing description of her car but was afraid, that if she did, he would re-open the question of money. So she allowed herself to be ushered outside. He wasn't driving the Cadillac, but a low-slung, open-topped Porsche. 'Hope you're not worried about the breeze in your hair?' he asked. 'If you are, I can put the top back up.'

'No, that's fine. I love it.' Gemma looked forward to the exhilaration of a drive with the wind whistling past her ears, and decided to be forgiving about his comments on the aged Lincoln. 'If this is another example of your vehicles, I'm not surprised you thought poorly of mine.'

Presently, he drew up in front of a garage, asked for her keys and swung his long legs out of the car. She watched him as he went in, talked to the man inside, and came back to her.

How loose-limbed and athletic his walk was!

'All arranged. He'll call, do what's necessary and leave the keys in your mail box for you.'

She suspected, from seeing the garage man's slightly obsequious attitude, when talking to Grant, that she was likely to be getting extra-special service. It didn't please her that her companion's position, and reputation, locally, would work to her advantage, but it didn't seem the moment to object to that.

When Grant slowed the Porsche and drew into the side five minutes later, Gemma gazed about her with a sharp sense of curiosity. By then, they had been climbing steadily on curving roads, and the only house in sight was an impressive, large, glass-and-timber one on three levels, built into the side of the hill, and slightly above them.

Grant looked sideways at her. 'That's the old homestead. Well, not exactly old — I only had it built three years ago, but I designed it myself with the help of an architect friend. We go in round the back, so I thought I'd let you have a look at it from here. I'm kind of proud of it.' He sounded as anxious for her approval as a six-year-old presenting his first painting.

Gemma could not say anything for a moment. The place was a dream. She had known he would have a fine house, but this — this was on the grand scale. Below it, the ground was level, jutting out from the hill. On the second floor were glass walls and wooden pillars, whilst, on the highest level a round, iron balcony followed the curve of the building. 'It's beautiful. You must have the most staggering view. I'm very impressed.'

Grant grinned. He seemed pleased by her praise.

'As you can see it's all wood, treated, not painted. You've probably noticed that we like the houses to blend in with the landscape around here. Every piece of timber came from my own trees.'

He started the engine again and they climbed a farther curve, coming around behind the house. Here the aspect was very different, with a tarmacadam road leading to a wide courtyard, where several other cars were already parked. As they purred to a halt beside a row of potted shrubs, the door was opened and Gemma saw a middle-aged, oriental woman holding it for them.

She extended her small hand in welcome, and Gemma took it. 'You're Miss Lawrence — Gemma.' The voice, though soft and well-modulated, was American. Her greeting was a statement rather than a question.

'Yes — and you?'

Grant answered for her. 'This is my Lotus Blossom.'

The woman laughed and gave him an admonitory slap on the arm. 'Don't take any notice of him. My family came from Thailand, but I have lived in the States all my life. My name is Aimee Lee. My husband, Ching Lee, and I take care of Grant. Believe me, it's not an easy job.'

Grant muttered, 'Thanks,' but she swept on.

'Please come this way. Sugar and Jim are down by the pool.'

She led the way through a large, windowed, lounge area, through a dining-room with a handsome kitchen off, and down some open stairs with an ironwork rail. Gemma had time only to gain quick impressions — like spaciousness, a velvety carpet underfoot, and a vast stonework fireplace on one curving wall. To her amazement, the next level took them through another lounge, another dining room, another kitchen, and a fully-fitted bar.

Grant, still close by, went straight to it. 'I'm going to mix you a long, cool drink,' he said. 'How about Kahlua and cream on the rocks?'

'Not yet, Grant.' Aimee sounded disapproving. 'Miss Lawrence will want to freshen up and change into her swim things.'

'Please, do call me Gemma.' She found it difficult, sorting out the social order of things. This woman seemed to be Grant's housekeeper, yet she spoke to him like a big sister, and was clearly on first name terms with all the family.

'Gemma, then. Just along here are some bedrooms and bathrooms. Please consider the Peacock Room yours for the day.'

Grant groaned. 'Oh, not the Peacock! Sugar went wild in that one, Gemma!'

Gemma followed Aimee through a door beside the bar and found herself in a circular corridor with four doors off. To her astonishment, each had the name of a bird on it. Passing the 'Eagle' and 'Swan' rooms, Aimee turned the brass doorknob of the 'Peacock'. 'You'll find a robe and plenty of towels. When you're ready come back to the bar. Grant, or I, will be there to take you to the pool.' With a smile, she left Gemma on her own.

'Wow!' Alone at last, Gemma could openly marvel at the luxury of her surroundings. She felt like a little country mouse. Flinging her shoulder bag, swimsuit and towel upon the king-sized bed, with its silken, peacock coverlet, she gazed at the myriad of golden lamps, opened the wide walk-in closets, all lined with peacock silk, and went into the ensuite bathroom.

'Good grief, I don't believe it,' she exclaimed as she spotted the taps, each one a small, gleaming peacock. 'It's pure Hollywood.'

Inwardly laughing, she slipped into her swim-suit, drew on the white robe laid ready, and went out into the corridor. Her bare feet made no sound on the thick carpet as she came to the door of the bar. Voices reached her from the other side. Hesitating to break in on a conversation, she heard her own name.

It was Grant's voice. 'Gemma refused. I hope it's not final. We've had too many years of waiting for the old lady, to give in now.'

Gemma felt as though a cold wave of

water had been flung over her. So warm when with her, so cool when talking about her. She pressed herself back against the wall and took deep, slow breaths to calm herself. The other speaker, she realised after a moment, was Jim.

He was agreeing with Grant that the situation was frustrating, but surely his friendship with the girl must make a difference? It was probably just a matter of time before the land became his. Gemma found she could not bear to hear the reply, and turned, edging back along the wall and into the bedroom.

When, later, she emerged again, she deliberately made the doorknob rattle and pushed the door behind her to close with a loud click. The murmur of voices stopped as she approached. Grant, smilingly, handed her a tall glass filled with a creamy liquid. The answering smile, with which she took it from him, was brittle-hard, and his own faded as he watched her.

'Jim, how nice to see you again. It's

been such a long time.' She sipped the
drink, aware that she sounded as false
as a talking doll, but not quite able to
behave normally. 'This is delicious,
Grant. Where's the pool then? I can
hardly wait to get in it,' she babbled.

Looking puzzled, Grant led the way
to a door. Stepping through, Gemma
saw that this wing was the one faced
with glass. Through the curved, patio
doors she saw, directly below them, a
large 'S' shaped swimming pool, flanked
by a Jacuzzi. The view, as she had
known it would be, was magnificent.

The plateau stretched for miles,
spread before them like a child's map.
Low clouds shrouded blue hills in the
distance and, below them, two little
boys splashed noisily in the water
watched by Sugar, on a lounger. She
patted the lounger beside her invitingly,
and called, 'Hi, Gemma. C'mon down.
I've just been dying to see you again.'

Have you, Gemma thought grimly.
Then why didn't you do something
about it? As she went down the iron

steps to pool level and across to where Sugar lay, she disliked both brother and sister equally impartially, hating herself for being in this idle, rich man's paradise. Why had she been so weak as to have accepted? But nothing of this showed on her face, as she took off her robe and lowered herself onto the lounger.

The boys, seeing Grant and their father, clambered out and dragged them back into the pool with them to play Tag with a big, coloured ball.

Alone with Sugar, Gemma waited.

'Gemma, I'm real sorry about your grandmother, but you did understand, didn't you?' Not feeling like making it easier for her, Gemma said nothing. Sugar floundered on. 'Grant's told you how it was, hasn't he?'

'Has he?' Gemma sipped her drink, remaining non-commital.

Sugar looked hurt and anxious. 'He told me that you knew about the way our family was on bad terms with your grandmother. And that it was kind of awkward for us when we found out who you were.'

Gemma was cool, keeping an invisible barrier between them. 'What I don't understand is how it all began. Why was my grandmother and her property such a thorn in your father's side?'

Although it had not become cooler, Sugar sat up and made a business of slipping on a wrap that hung over the back of her chair. There was a flustered look on her face and, when she spoke, it was more slowly than usual. 'You've sort of hit me with this one, Gemma. I thought you and Grant had talked about it.'

'No, we haven't.' Gemma felt some compunction when she saw the unhappy look that was evident on Sugar's face.

'The problem is, that if I tell you, straight out, what we've always known — believed — it sounds kind of — like I'm slanging your grandmother.'

'I see.' Gemma drained her drink and

stood up, saying evenly, 'If that's the case, perhaps you'd better not say any more. Shall we go into the water?'

Sugar's expression lightened at being allowed to drop the subject. She put out a restraining hand. 'No, wait a while. Tell me first how you and my kid brother are getting along. I guess he's really smitten with you.'

Gemma said lightly, 'He's been very kind.'

Sugar probed a little more. 'How do you feel about him?'

Gemma did not wish to be cross-examined about her relationship with Grant. Glad of her sun-glasses, she turned away and watched the group in the pool without answering.

After a moment, Sugar hurried on. 'Well, if it's a character reference Grant needs, I can sure give him one. He's the biggest philanthropist in this district, he's underwritten every struggling, small business that ever started round here. I reckon the hospitals and schools would be in trouble without his help

— in fact, this town would fall apart if Grant didn't keep shoring things up.'

'Really?' Gemma, though intensely interested, was still acutely embarrassed by what Sugar was saying. Judging it wiser to hear no more, she suggested they join the others, and the next hour was spent in the blue water. After that, whenever Grant spoke to her or swam with her, she was aware of his sister's eyes on them.

However, when lunch was served in the room containing the bar, she had regained her natural warmth, and felt ashamed of having listened and reacted to a conversation she was not intended to hear.

Grant was a good host, attentive and teasing. She decided he was at his best here, both as an employer, a brother and an uncle. She told him so, and thanked him, as he drove her home through the evening light, and drew up close to the steps of her house.

As the engine died, he said quietly, 'I'm glad you had a good day, Gemma.'

His look was intense and Gemma did not try to break the spell as he leaned forward and took her chin in his hand. In a conversational tone, he said softly, 'I'm going to kiss you. Do you mind?'

Mutely, Gemma shook her head. By then, his face was very close and she thought he smiled, but could not be sure — all thoughts were suspended as pure sensation began to take her over.

His seeking mouth moved from her face to her neck, to her bare shoulders, as his equally-demanding hands held her to him. Gemma began to be enveloped in a state of delicious lethargy. Eyes closed, she gave herself up to the pleasure of his nearness. Still together, he eased her out of the car until they stood on the deck. It was as though she had no will of her own, and was powerless to prevent their mutual, growing passion.

Suddenly, with a loud screeching, a blue jay flew from one of the trees close to the cabin. Grant stilled and raised his head. Gemma, her lips still against his neck, was aware of his changed mood, his inattentiveness. 'What is it? What's wrong?'

'This is.' Grant's voice was flat and definite. The light was failing now and, in the semi-darkness, Gemma looked up searchingly, trying to see his expression.

'This?' she repeated, wonderingly. 'I don't know what you mean.'

Grant sighed, gently disengaging himself and setting her away from him. As their bodies parted, even though he was only a foot away, Gemma felt appallingly alone.

He spoke rapidly. 'I think I love you. I know that I want you — very much.' He held his hands out in a helpless gesture and then dropped them to his sides, looking defeated. 'But I know, that if we make love tonight, it doesn't answer anything. Do you trust me?'

Into her head came small memories. 'Never trust a Markham'. Who said that? Then that cool voice earlier in the day. 'We've had too many years of waiting for the old lady to give in now.'

Suddenly tears pricked her eyes. Why could she not simply hold out her arms to him and give him an unqualified answer, when she wanted to so much? He would have stayed with her, and held her close throughout the long, lonely night. But she was too honest. 'I want to trust you,' she cried. 'I really do.'

He waited, tall, stern and rigid in the moonlight, until Gemma, driven to tears and not wishing him to see, stumbled up the steps away from him. There was a long pause. Would he come after her?

Then, setting the seal on her misery, she heard the car springing into life. He had gone — and she was once more alone.

9

Two days later, when Grant rang and reminded Gemma that he was taking her to the mountains for the day, she would have agreed to go with him had he been Quasimodo himself. Loneliness was a very real thing, she had discovered, and no matter how she kept it at bay with work, there came a time when there were no more chores that needed doing, and one faced up to one's own company.

She decided that the trip to the mountains would be a welcome break. Even to herself, she did not admit that seeing Grant again was the icing on the cake. She was determined to try and forget their last emotional scene. Just enjoy his company, she told herself; he'd obviously accepted her refusal to sell, so there was no reason at all to turn down a day out.

She took trouble choosing what she should wear. It was still hot by day, and it seemed wise to wear something light and cool. Thong sandals, brief, coral-coloured shorts and top, were what she eventually decided upon. But she took a track suit and stout shoes as well, in case it got cooler on higher ground.

When Grant arrived, he was in the Cadillac. After one look at her, he said positively, 'You'll need some warmer clothes. We shall be out for several hours and, by evening, the temperature up in the Cascades is very different from the heat down here on the plateau.'

Gemma smiled and held up her bag. 'All accounted for,' she said smugly, as she slid into the luxurious car, beside him. He smiled back. Good, she thought, it looks as though we've both come to the same decision — to enjoy one another's company and not to agonise about the past or the feud.

As they entered the Cascade foot-hills, the road was a curling series of hairpin bends. On Grant's side, as the car went higher and higher, they began to see the tops of the tall, fir trees that filled the gorges and canyons below, whilst up above, there were yet more, all pointing to the clear blue sky.

Grant pointed out three mountains in the distance which he said were called the Three Sisters. Each of them, in all the warmth of the day, still had a snow-capped peak.

He said, 'I'm taking you to my cabin. It's where we go to ski in the winter, but even in the summer, I think you'll like it.'

Within a mile or so the land began to level out and, when they rounded the next bend, there was a lake before them, a blue jewel of tranquillity and calm. Grant eased the car in amongst the trees and, when he turned off the engine, the silence was immense. The only sound was a distant one of crashing water where a waterfall, on the other side of the lake, dropped into it. He got out and came round to open the door.

'Thank you,' she murmured as she got out, aware of the presence of his hand on hers. He did not let go. As casually as though they always walked hand in hand, he led her away from the car, taking a path down towards the lakeside.

'Fantastic,' Gemma breathed, when they stood side by side on the wooden planking which served as a landing stage for the occasional, small, fishing boat. It's beautiful, the most peaceful scene I've ever encountered.'

He looked pleased and he lifted the hand he held, dropping a light kiss on it. Gemma felt stunned. How could he make such easy, nonchalant, loving gestures if he didn't mean them? Unable to snatch away her hand, she was totally nonplussed.

'Grant, please, don't do that,' she faltered.

'What's the matter?' He seemed

genuinely puzzled. 'It was just a little 'Thank you' for admiring the beauties of Diamond Lake, and the North West, as much as I do.'

'How could I do anything else,' she cried, 'when there's a glorious sight like this in front of me?'

They drove on for another three quarters of an hour, through breathtaking scenery. Grant said at one point, 'I'm hoping these mists will clear for your first, clear sight of the mountain.'

'The mountain?' Gemma asked, slightly puzzled.

'Yes. The one near the cabin. The one we call our mountain — Woodman's Peak. Keep your eyes peeled now, Gemma. I don't want you to miss it.'

She had not noticed the mist swirling above but realised now that the tops of the tallest trees were obscured by low-lying cloud. They passed a few scattered cabins, and a store with a hitching post outside, rather like something out of a cowboy film.

'That's THE store,' Grant said with a

grin. 'It's really old-fashioned. Sells everything they need round here — which is just as well, otherwise they'd have a long trip to the nearest town.'

As they drove past, Gemma looked up at a bird she thought was a hawk or an eagle and, because she was looking straight up, caught her first glimpse of Woodman's Peak. 'Grant, look, look,' she breathed in wonder. 'It's up in the sky.'

The mountain had appeared through the clouds, the sun glistening on its top, gleaming whitely above the shawl of fog around its shoulders. 'It's like a vision,' she whispered. 'I never expected it to be so high — and so close.'

'I know,' Grant agreed, well-pleased with her awed reaction. 'If she's coyly hiding in the clouds, no-one ever expects her to pop her head out like that. We all feel the same when we first see it.'

Gemma realised again how tied to the land he was, how much this place meant to him. Though it reinforced some of her fears, it cleared a few, to know that he had brought her there to share it. Surely, some of his feelings were genuine if he wanted her to know the places he loved so much.

When they got to the cabin, Gemma saw it was almost hidden amongst the trees. Grant stopped the car on the track and Gemma's soft exclamation of pleasure seemed to be all he needed.

'Like it?' he asked, but her face was enough to give him his answer.

The sleek Cadillac, which had carried them so smoothly over the winding, climbing terrain, now seemed incongruously modern, parked in front of the little, wooden house perched so cosily amongst the trees and dwarfed by the majestic giants all around.

They walked up and stepped onto the platform deck where a big, log pile nestled. Grant inserted a key into the door and ushered Gemma in ahead of him into a huge, high-ceilinged room. It held a chimneyed woodstove and two couches on the left, and an old-fashioned dining table with six, carved chairs on the right. Ahead of them was a serviceable-looking kitchen and, from it, led a staircase.

'Every single thing is wood; roof, floors and walls!' Gemma gasped.

'And all from our own trees,' Grant answered with the pride that always came into his voice at the mention of his trees. 'I'll light the wood stove — it makes a nice glow, though, of course, we don't need it on a day like this.'

He quickly fetched some logs, opened the glass door, and set them alight, before saying, 'Come out the back,' and leading the way through to a back door which opened onto another deck with a sunken hot tub off it.

'In winter,' he said, 'there's absolutely nothing like rolling in the snow and then getting straight back into the hot tub, with a glass of something warming.'

Gemma felt a rush of longing. To do these things with Grant would be like Heaven, she thought. It came to her there, standing with him in his little, wooden house — a total conviction that she had fallen hopelessly in love. From now on, a world without Grant Markham, a future that did not hold his presence, would be bleak and empty. This astonishing knowledge bemused her so much that she followed him on his guided tour of the two bedrooms and bathrooms without really seeing anything — not the Indian carvings, not the rough paintings on the wall, nor the thick ethnic rugs.

Once, she shivered from her own inner turmoil and Grant said remorsefully, 'You're cold. Go, sit by the stove and I'll fetch in our picnic.'

Obediently, Gemma went and perched on one of the couches, glad to have a moment to reflect on the amazing certainty that she loved him — desperately, and for ever. Why, why, why, she thought desolately. Why does it have to be fraught with the aftermath of this beastly feud? How will I ever know if he likes me for myself? Why can't it be straightforward?

Grant took no more than a couple of minutes to bring in a big basket and put it down on the dining room table. Once opened, it was revealed as a cool-box; and Gemma watched, unbelievingly, as he first produced a bottle of champagne, and a whole, foil-wrapped, fresh salmon.

'It's a feast, not a picnic,' she said, trying to be light-hearted.

With a flourish, he fetched two tall, green glasses from a cupboard, popped the champagne cork, and quickly handed her the first glass.

'To us,' he said, looking deep into her eyes.

How much I wish I could honestly echo the toast, Gemma thought, as she sipped appreciatively.

'To us,' she murmured self-consciously, eyes downcast.

Grant saw her hesitation, and a small frown appeared on his forehead, but he said nothing. Instead, he threw himself into becoming the attentive host,

181

offering her the delicate fish, pâté, biscuits and salad until she was replete.

'Nothing must go back, unless you want to hurt Aimee's feelings,' he insisted, though there was far more than the two of them could eat.

Later, sated with food and drink, he led her on a hike through the sun-dappled forest at the back, almost to the foot of Woodman's Peak. Gemma, walking behind him along the narrow trail, was glad of her track suit and sensible shoes. The sun was not strong, and the trail was used more by animals than by people.

She wondered, apprehensively, if bears were in the vicinity, but didn't feel like asking Grant and exposing her ignorance. It would be easy to imagine a big, brown bear emerging from behind any of the trees, it was so quiet, still and mysterious.

When they reached the foot of the mountain, Grant stopped and flung himself full length on a patch of grass. 'Well done.' He smiled at her. 'You've kept up well, and I'm afraid I set a cracking pace — or so my nephews tell me.'

She smiled back. 'Yes, you do. It's lucky I'm reasonably fit.' Fit or not, she was glad to plump down on the dry grass beside him.

Neither of them spoke for a few minutes, as they rested and drank in the soft, forest sounds around them. It was Grant who broke the idyll. His voice, after the companionable pleasures of the day, sounded cold, as though he was saying something he was forcing himself into.

'I'm in love with you,' he said baldly. 'Will you marry me?'

'Please don't, Grant,' she pleaded. 'I'm flattered, of course, and grateful. But I can't make that kind of decision here — now — yet.'

'Why can't you make any decision?'

'Because we hardly know each other.' From the depths of her confusion, her voice, too, sounded far more distant and detached than she felt.

'All right, if hardly knowing each other is the only objection, that can be remedied.' Abruptly, he sat up. Before she fully comprehended his intentions, he had grabbed her and was kissing her, his arms locked tightly round her waist.

Gemma knew she had two options — to melt into his embrace as she wanted to do — or to fight him off. She chose the latter option. The minute he released her and sat back, breathing faster, she hit out at him with her fists. 'Let me go. I didn't come with you today for this.'

'Didn't you? Then why come at all?'

He didn't look like or sound like the Grant she knew. Seeing only that he had become cold and implacable, Gemma was too angry and shaken to recognise hurt rejection when she saw it. Struggling to her feet, she began to run back along the trail, scrambling through briars and bushes.

Ignoring his cry of 'Gemma, wait!' she plunged through the undergrowth, conscious only of the need to get away from those hard, blue eyes, and the icy, hateful person he had become.

After a while, saner counsel prevailed and she slowed down. He, too, was crashing through dry branches and tangled creepers behind her, in order to catch up — and he was gaining on her. Calm down, she told herself. Be sensible. You have to face him, because there's no other way to get home than in his car. Turning, she stood stock-still and waited for him to come.

He, too, stood still a few yards away and faced her, eyeing her uneasily. Both of them, by this time, were panting. Like antagonists, combatants, they faced each other a short distance apart.

Grant said unevenly, 'Since it appears to have upset you so much, I apologise — although for what I'm not certain.'

Gemma spoke quickly. 'I'm sorry, too. Could we please forget the whole thing, and go back to the way we were before?'

He nodded, a cool, accepting little nod. Her heart was wrenched again at

185

the change in him. He was no longer her Grant, the one she had fallen in love with. In his place stood this blond stranger, who looked like him, but who had erected a barrier between them — a barrier she dare not even attempt to break through.

10

If Gemma had hoped to hear from Grant once she was home again — and she would not admit to herself that she did — the hope was doomed to disappointment. After three days of silence, she was nearly at screaming pitch.

One minute she was angrily certain he was leaving her alone to teach her a lesson, the next she was feeling guiltily sorry that she had not been able to lie.

Would it have cost her so much to tell him that she trusted him absolutely? Gemma, who was nothing if not honest, knew that she could not have made such an assurance if she did not feel it. But even knowing that, did not stop her longing to. It would have made life so much simpler to have no nagging doubts; to see him as the secure protector he seemed.

The only good thing that happened during those three days was the arrival of the old car, punctiliously delivered to her door with the keys. When asked what had been wrong, the garage men were vague, saying, 'Everything's all sorted out now,' and waved aside her attempts to pay them with a laconic, 'Mr Markham's settled all that.'

On the fourth day, she awoke to the horrifying fact that she was not as alone as she thought.

Little noises, creaks and small sounds, the closing of a door she could not remember opening, had made her jumpy. She had dismissed them as her own overstretched imagination, but when she sat up in bed that morning and heard the closing of the sliding, patio door below, it had become a frightening certainty. Someone was there.

The fear that, whoever it was, had come into the house, and would be coming upstairs, kept her rigidly immobile for precious moments before an unexpected noise outside reached her straining ears. Running! Someone had dashed across the wooden veranda and was now crashing through trees and undergrowth.

Cross with herself for not having thought of the possibility that someone was leaving rather than entering, Gemma got quickly to her feet and ran to the window. By then, there was nothing to be seen, as she had known there would not be.

Shakily, she pulled on a robe and cautiously pulled open the door, still half-afraid of finding a man outside. The house was empty. She went over it, from room to room, and satisfied herself she was, indeed, the only occupant. It was worrying that the back door was unlocked — she was almost sure she had locked it before going to bed.

After she had re-locked both doors and dressed, Gemma made herself a cup of coffee. She had to think — but her brain felt like cotton wool! The first thing to consider was that the intruder had not tried to be stealthy about leaving. The door had slammed back, and the footsteps had been loud.

That meant he was not trying to hide from her, that he wanted her to hear him — but not see him. Why? After some intense soul-searching, she came to the painful conclusion that it was someone trying to frighten her, someone she knew, which narrowed the field considerably. But who would want to frighten her deliberately? And why?

An immediate instinct had to be to ring Grant but, even as her hand went to the telephone, she snatched it back. How would she get the truth that way? He would probably come and he would probably be soothing, but would she ever know whether he had been the prowler? After all, he was the one who wanted her out! He hadn't been able to buy her out — maybe, now, he thought he could frighten her out. Her brain went round and round in circles.

Preparing her meal, as the dusk

closed in outside, was a time of nerve-racking anxiety. Tell herself as she would that everything was locked; and she had done this a hundred times without incident, her ears and eyes were still attuned to the slightest sound. The television failed, miserably, to distract her.

Trying to read in bed, the words of print had no meaning and, when she eventually turned out her lamp and lay down, her eyes refused to close, but stared anxiously into the moonlit darkness.

It was not long before she heard what she dreaded — the sound of a key being turned, a footfall, a weight on the floor below. She recognised, with her heart in her mouth, the familiar creak of the uneven board in the kitchen. Someone was there. She was certain of it.

Thankful that she had had the foresight to drag a chest of drawers across the door, she reached for the bedside phone extension she'd put in. She had decided that when she was sure someone had broken in, she would ring Grant. If he were out, it proved nothing. But if he were in, it proved his innocence. She wanted that so much — even more than getting the police there.

The ringing seemed to go on for hours but, when he answered, even in her fear, she knew a fierce joy. So it was not him. 'Grant, it's Gemma. I'm really frightened — there's an intruder in the cabin.'

Even though she was whispering, he took in the situation immediately. 'Can you barricade yourself in?'

'I've done that already.'

'Hang on, darling. I'll be right there.'

The 'darling' was as heartening as his decisive voice had been. The phone had already gone dead, but the ping of the receiver being put down seemed as though it echoed through the house. Gemma reached for her grandmother's stick — she'd placed it beside the bed. If he came up — and she guessed now who it was — she must use it to defend herself. There were more sounds.

He was moving about, touching, looking, not even troubling to be overly quiet. He must be very sure of himself, she thought, surprised. But then, he probably didn't know about the bed-room telephone; that was a fairly new innovation.

In one way she was still sorry for him, still pitied him. Because, of course, it was Matt Fulton. He was touching and looking at things in a proprietorial way, because he believed everything should belong to him — including her. That thought was blood-curdling.

If he came up, dare she hope that she would have the power over him that she had had the last time? She doubted it. 'Oh, Grant,' she whispered under her breath, 'please get here quickly.'

The handle of the door turned and it opened a crack before he discovered the barricade. He gave a roar of anger, knowing then that there was no sleeping girl inside, but that she was awake and aware. The chest was heavy, and moving. It gave him enough trouble to give her time to run and stand behind the door. She clicked on the light before raising the walking stick over her head with both hands. She felt, instinctively, that it would be better to see him, rather than face an assailant whose face was hidden in darkness.

Matt's gasps of effort, as he finally forced open the door, were horrifying, like the sounds an animal might make. At first, he headed for the empty bed, then turned and saw her. Gemma said, as steadily as she could get the words out, 'Don't come any nearer. If you do, I'll bring this stick down on your head.'

Keep him talking, Gemma thought frantically. Say anything. 'Why are you here?' she said icily. 'You have no right . . . '

'No right, eh?' He was scathing. 'This oughta been my place — I was cheated. And since you're the one that did the cheating, I guess you're the one who's gonna pay.'

Gemma, watching his face, knew that

talking would do no good. It was then that he decided to lunge at her. She was ready though, and brought the stick down with all of her might, closing her eyes against the sight. But Matt was too quick for her. The stick only hit him on his burly shoulder.

He gasped and staggered, but it did no more than halt him for a moment. With a sinking heart, Gemma realised that all her brave stand had done was anger him. He gave another roar, this time of mingled pain and fury, and held onto his injured shoulder, his eyes never leaving her. Then, he moved forward again and plucked the stick from her as though it had been a matchstick.

Fearfully, she watched her last line of defence being hurled across the room, as Matt brought himself up to press her against the wall. She was as helpless as a bird in a trap.

Suddenly, miraculously he was plucked away. Mercifully saved, Gemma did not, for a second, realise what had happened until gasps and grunts filled the room, and she saw who had come up and torn Matt from her.

'Grant,' she whispered, suddenly fearful for him, as she watched the two men fight. He was so much lighter than Matt. Remorse came, then. If she had not doubted him, he would not be in this danger now — because she would have called the police instead of him. Fearfully, she watched, and gradually confidence came and relief washed over her as she saw the younger, more agile man, gaining the upper hand.

Matt was being driven against the door. One well-aimed punch sent him out on to the gallery, where he lost his footing and tumbled over the top step, crashing head over heels down the rest of the wooden staircase. From the bottom, spreadeagled and winded, he gazed malevolently up at the panting Grant, silhouetted in the pool of light from the bedroom.

'You'll be sorry for this, Markham,' he shouted, scrambling painfully to his feet. 'I'll make sure of that.'

Gemma ran to Grant, whose arm came round and clasped her to him. Together, they watched silently after the shambling, limping figure as he disappeared through the patio door and out into the night and the forest. Then, at last, reaction set in.

Turning into Grant's arms, Gemma burst into tears. Even then, sobbing gustily as she was, she felt secure, as though she had finally come home. Over her head, he was saying soothing things she hardly heard, because, most of all, his arms meant safety. Safety that she could now, thankfully, accept and believe in.

Presently, when she had had her cry, they drew, reluctantly apart. Grant looked lovingly down at her. 'We need to talk. Do you want to know what the feud was all about?'

Gemma sniffed. 'Yes, please, but let me get dressed. Go down and make some coffee while I'm getting presentable.'

Once settled downstairs with a

steaming mug of coffee in her hand, she asked Grant to sit in the other chair so that, as she explained, 'I won't be distracted from all the things we have to say.'

He smiled and complied, but told her, seriously, that she might not like it.

'I've gone through all the records with a fine toothcomb, and I can't hide it from you, Gemma. The means by which Ruth Lawrence, your grand-mother, acquired the land was legal — but only just! Matt Fulton was able, because he worked for us in those days, to engineer the whole thing.

'He was later sacked, not for that, but for a number of things. He couldn't get the land deed in his own name, but he got it in hers — until then, she'd only been a tenant.

'There had been collusion of some kind, but how much we'll never know.'

Gemma was painfully silent for a while, gazing down into her coffee cup. Finally, she sighed and said, 'I believe you. It makes sense. But I won't ever believe she was knowingly fraudulent — though it's another reason why Matt's twisted mind reckoned on the land being rightfully his. But if you think I'm going to let it cloud my memories of my grandmother, you're wrong. All I remember — all I'm going to remember — is her kindness, and that she loved me very much.'

'Good girl,' Grant approved. 'But now to us. When can you marry me? Tomorrow? The next day? Next week?'

'What kind of proposal is that?' She laughed, secretly thrilled by his impatience. 'Anyway, be serious for a minute. You know I can't keep this place now. It wouldn't feel right. Can you organise the lawyers so that I can hand it back to you officially?'

'No, I can't.' In his vehemence, Grant almost shouted the words. 'Don't be absurd, Gemma. Even if you managed that, I should give it back to you — as a wedding present,' he concluded.

Grant suddenly stiffened. He was looking at the window.

'Grant, what's wrong?' Gemma became aware of her rigidity. 'Is he back?' She looked fearfully at the uncurtained glass and saw what Grant had seen. An ominous red glow in the night sky.

He said, 'It's a fire. Near my place, maybe on it. And everything's been tinder dry for weeks! I'll have to go, darling, right away. And I'm not leaving you here alone now. So come on.'

He was urging her towards the door and Gemma, picking up only her bag and a warm jacket, followed him. Would this night of drama never end, she thought, as she sat beside a grim-faced Grant and sped off into the night.

As he drove in the direction of the red glow, Gemma said tentatively, 'If it's on your land, do you think this is what Matt meant when he said you'd pay?'

'I'm sure of it.' Grant was terse, intent on this thoughts and his driving. 'But forest fires are devastating. To start one deliberately is an unforgivable thing to do. We get some every year about this time and getting them controlled quickly is vital.' They heard the shrieking of sirens, and Grant's anxious face cleared a little. 'At least the fire-fighters are on their way,' he said. 'And those guys really know their business.'

Grant drew up in the back drive of the house. Before he had even inserted his key in the door, Aimee, looking, for her, very agitated, had opened the door. 'Oh, Grant, I'm so glad you're back. What must I do?'

Her eyes widened as she saw Gemma behind him, and Grant said, 'Nothing, for the moment — except look after Gemma for me. I've got to go — but first I'm going to ring the fire-fighting unit of my loggers and get them out here. They may not have seen the fire from town, but I've got a nucleus of men and equipment always ready to mobilise.'

Gemma said, 'I'm coming with you,' but he was firm in his refusal to let her.

'No, you're not. You're staying here,' He came up, held her by the shoulders and looked into her face. 'Understand, darling, that I can't be worrying about you, too. I have to do this, knowing that you're safe.'

'Are we safe here?' Aimee asked. Her bright, knowing eyes had widened at the obvious fact of the changed relationship and the 'darling'.

'Yes, for the forseeable future. There's a dry wind from the canyon, and that will push the fire up in a northern direction. It's bound to be spreading that way, but if anything changes, I'll come straight back and get you away.'

'All right.' Gemma was docile, seeing the logic in what he said, and resolving that, if she couldn't help, at least she wouldn't hinder. 'But please be careful, won't you?'

'Of course. You don't think I've found you, only for us to lose each other again, do you? I'll take no unnecessary risks.' He smiled, but she could see that he was anxious to get into the action, to save his beloved trees, and said no more to hold him up.

Left alone, the two women looked at each other. 'It's my fault,' Gemma said unhappily. 'Or, at least, it's because of me.'

Aimee reverted to her usual, brisk self at this. 'I'm sure it's nothing of the sort,' she said. 'Anyway, it's no use worrying — leave it all to Grant. If you want something to do, help me get out some cups and make drinks. The firemen will probably come back here for rest periods, and we'd better be prepared.'

Gemma suspected that she was being kept deliberately busy to prevent her giving way to anxiety but, in the event, Aimee was proved right. Within an hour, a jeep-load of men arrived, all with blackened faces and reddened eyes.

Throughout the night, this procedure was followed no less than three times. Whenever the two women had re-equipped the bathrooms with towels, and had made another supply of coffee and sandwiches, a team of four arrived.

Aimee appeared unruffled by this dramatic change in routine but Gemma, whilst trying not to show it, was beginning to feel wilted by three o'clock.

With the fourth batch came good news. They had contained the blaze and, providing it was watched, it could now be allowed to burn itself out in safety. Grant would be on his way shortly, they said, before making their 'Goodbyes' and leaving for their respective homes.

Gemma's heart leaped with relief. He had been in the thick of it, they'd told her, directing operations, tireless in the organisation of men and supplies. Each time they'd appeared, she'd dreaded the news of an accident involving him — had visions of burning trees falling on him before she'd had time to tell him she loved him. That would have been unbearable irony.

The last man had driven away minutes before Grant appeared. He looked exhausted, his face more sombre than she had ever seen it. Wordlessly, she went into his arms, heedless of blackening her clothes. Like the others, he smelled of charred-wood smoke.

'It's controlled now,' he said heavily, 'and we've got to be thankful there's been no loss of life. We've left the freshest team in charge, but it raged like a fury.

'The trees went up like matches, just a flare to their branches and the next moment — pouf — they were a pyramid of fire.'

'I'm sorry,' she whispered, but he didn't seem to hear.

His eyes were inwardly focussed: he still had to talk about it. 'Thank goodness for the river. It made a natural boundary on one side. We dropped retardant all around in a triangle, and built fortified lines to contain the spread. We managed to stop it within a mile of a fallen timber area — we had to do that because when fire gets into a downed piece, it really goes.'

'Grant,' Gemma said steadily, interrupting the flow. 'Please stop thinking about it. It's over. Please come back to me.' Her whole self pitied his vulnerability, his distress at the damage to his trees, and she longed to comfort him. His face changed then, as though seeing her for the first time, but still his smile was not the confident, arrogant smile she was used to. It was a twisted, loving one.

'What an idiot I am,' he said. 'Look, darling, I can't sleep yet. This night is a write-off anyway. Give me time to shower and I'll be back with you — a changed man in every way.'

Aimee, with quiet efficiency and apparent tirelessness, produced yet more coffee and sandwiches as soon as he reappeared. He was looking more like himself, in crisp jeans and a white shirt. Then, with a sidelong, conspiratorial look at Gemma, she announced, 'Nothing is going to keep me from my bed any longer. Tell the next team of fire fighters to go elsewhere. Goodnight.'

'Goodnight, Aimee, and thanks for everything.' He stood up to kiss her on the cheek, but his eyes were now for Gemma. As soon as Aimee had disappeared, he came to her and took her in his arms.

Gemma, relaxing directly into his embrace, heard him murmur into the dark curls at her neck, 'Well, darling from the way I feel about you, and the stupid family feud, I think we might be Romeo and Juliet.' He pulled her back to look laughingly down at her, adding, 'Only please don't ask me to climb a balcony — I'm far too bushed.'

Gemma, too, dissolved into laughter. It was so good to be in his arms, so good to have his strength back and hear his flippancy. Trying to sound soulful, she asked solemnly, 'Could you manage a love song then, to serenade me?'

Abruptly, Grant let her go, flung wide his arms and cleared his throat. The noise that came out was reminiscent of a scrub jay. Hastily, stifling giggles, she put his arms back round her again and said, 'No I can't ask it of you, but if you can't do a little thing like that, are you sure this is true love?'

Gazing full into the eyes that now gazed, seriously, back into hers, Gemma said softly, 'You don't have to answer that, I know it is.'

Grant brought his mouth gently down on hers and said, just before their lips met, 'It really is, darling. For ever and ever.'

Gemma still wanted the last word and she pushed aside his eager mouth just long enough to say, a little breathlessly, 'And so they lived happily ever after.'

THE END

We do hope that you have enjoyed reading this large print book.

Did you know that all of our titles are available for purchase?

We publish a wide range of high quality large print books including:
Romances, Mysteries, Classics
General Fiction
Non Fiction and Westerns

Special interest titles available in large print are:
The Little Oxford Dictionary
Music Book, Song Book
Hymn Book, Service Book

Also available from us courtesy of Oxford University Press:
Young Readers' Dictionary
(large print edition)
Young Readers' Thesaurus
(large print edition)

For further information or a free brochure, please contact us at:
Ulverscroft Large Print Books Ltd.,
The Green, Bradgate Road, Anstey,
Leicester, LE7 7FU, England.
Tel: (00 44) **0116 236 4325**
Fax: (00 44) **0116 234 0205**

Other titles in the
Linford Romance Library:

VISIONS OF THE HEART

Christine Briscomb

When property developer Connor Grant contracted Natalie Jensen to landscape the grounds of his large country house near Ashley in South Australia, she was ecstatic. But then she discovered he was acquiring — and ripping apart — great swathes of the town. Her own mother's house and the hall where the drama group met were two of his targets. Natalie was desperate to stop Connor's plans — but she also had to fight the powerful attraction flowing between them.